KU-309-910

WHERE WE BELONG

Blamed for his sister's tragic death, estranged from his family, and his career in tatters, American Broadway singing star Liam Delaroche travels to Trelanow in Cornwall, searching for a new life. Meanwhile, local school-teacher Ellie Teague is on a mission to establish her independence after jilting Will, her longtime fiancé. The attraction between the two is instant and electric. But the shadow of Liam's past looms over their growing re-lationship — and then the first of his bitter family members shows up in Trelanow . . .

ANGELA BRITNELL

◆

WHERE WE BELONG

Complete and Unabridged

LINFORD
Leicester

First published in Great Britain in 2016

First Linford Edition
published 2017

Copyright © 2016 by Angela Britnell
All rights reserved

A catalogue record for this book is available
from the British Library.

ISBN 978–1–4448–3434–5

Published by
F. A. Thorpe (Publishing)
Anstey, Leicestershire

Set by Words & Graphics Ltd.
Anstey, Leicestershire
Printed and bound in Great Britain by
T. J. International Ltd., Padstow, Cornwall

This book is printed on acid-free paper

STAFFORDSHIRE
LIBRARIES, ARTS
AND ARCHIVES

0460394472

ULVERSCROFT   22 MAR 2018

F   £8.99

1

A deserted Cornish beach on a chilly, grey March afternoon wasn't everyone's idea of a perfect place to walk, but the bleakness suited Liam's unsettled mood. He tugged an old black woolly hat down over his ears and stuck his cold hands deep into his jeans pockets. Wandering down to the water's edge, he stared out over the blurred horizon, and an unexpected wave splashed over the top of his ragged trainers.

'If you're going paddling you ought to take your shoes off first.'

Liam spun around. 'Where did you spring from?'

'Sorry, I didn't mean to scare you. Next time I'll blow a whistle to announce my presence.' The young woman's eyes sparkled with amusement and Liam couldn't help noticing they were the searing hot blue of a summer sky. He'd

1

love to capture her expressive features on canvas: the drift of freckles sprinkled over her clear skin; a mouth too wide for conventional beauty. He'd set free the thick plait of dark gold hair and fan it out over her shoulders.

You don't paint anymore. Remember? The same way you've stopped doing everything else you love.

'If you'll excuse me, I'll continue with my walk before I freeze to death.' His grouchy response made the corners of her lips turn up again. 'And yeah, I know I should've worn a coat.'

'I'm no better.' She pointed to the baggy bright red jumper skimming her hips. 'Although I did have the sense to put on my boots.' Her matching scarlet Wellingtons almost drew a smile out of him. 'It's none of my business what you wear. My mother's always telling me to keep my nose out of other people's affairs.'

'I'm guessin' you don't take much notice?'

'Not as much as I should,' she

admitted with a slight shrug. 'I came down to the beach for a quiet walk and should've realised you were doing the same. A tactful person would've left you alone.'

'You don't fall into that category?'

She rolled her eyes. 'What do you think?'

'I think we haven't been properly introduced.' He stuck out his hand. 'Liam Delaroche at your service, ma'am.' As their hands connected, he fought the conflicting urges tugging at him. The sensible one told him to pull away as fast as possible, but he ignored it, savouring the surprising warmth from the woman's touch as long as possible before forcing himself to let go.

'Ellie Teague.'

'You're local?' He'd picked up on her soft Cornish accent immediately.

'Yes.' She turned around to point at the steep hill leading away from the harbour. 'The blue house halfway up on the right. That's the Teague madhouse.' Ellie's casual reference to her home struck a bleak chord inside him. 'Where's home for you? I'll take a wild guess you're the American staying in Mrs. Pascoe's old cottage. I heard it'd been rented while the family decide whether or not to sell.' She launched into a long rambling story about old Mrs. Pascoe, who'd passed away at Christmas after celebrating her hundredth birthday. 'They say she was found in her chair the morning after the party with an open bottle of champagne on the table next to her and an empty glass in her hand.' Ellie smiled. 'That's the way I'd like to go.'

To Liam's chagrin, he couldn't take his eyes off her.

Ellie slapped her hand over her mouth. 'There I go again. I never even gave you a chance to answer.'

'What was the question?' Liam cracked a smile.

'Home.'

'Nowhere, and everywhere. Creole father. Irish mother. I was born in New Orleans but I've lived all over the place.

Los Angeles. Madrid. Paris. New York.'
Liam shoved his hands back in his
pockets. 'I'd better be going. It was
good to meet you. Maybe I'll see you
around.'

'Trelanow is a small village. You'll
have to work hard to avoid me.'

'We'll see about that, won't we,
darlin'.' Liam gave her a teasing wink
and strode off, wondering what on
earth had just got into him.

★　★　★

The out-of-the-blue wink and Liam's
mischievous smile had tilted Ellie's
world off balance. They altered Liam's
severe appearance in the same way as
an unexpected splash of sunlight in a
dark room. His face was too long and
lean to be truly handsome, and the
slash of his dark eyebrows contrasted
with skin so pale he could've been a
ghost. Blue bruises of exhaustion cast
shadows under his deep-set dark eyes,
and Liam's faded black jeans and slate

grey jumper hung off his tall, bony frame. But something about him drew her against her better judgement.

For goodness sake, Ellie, don't pick up any more strays. Will's criticism rang in her ears but she shut it out. Never again would she let anyone tell her how much or how little to feel. It'd caused more than a few raised eyebrows when she left her fiancé standing at the altar, but she had no regrets.

Ellie took her time walking home, and as she fitted her key in the lock her mother jerked open the front door. 'Get in here, you silly girl. Look at you. You're soaked.'

If she said she hadn't noticed the heavy drizzle, her mother would mark her down as crazy, so Ellie held her tongue and submitted to being pulled into the hall and fussed over.

'Why didn't you wear a sensible raincoat or carry an umbrella? Anyone would think you were five years old.' Jennifer Teague shook her head in disgust. She steered Ellie to sit down and tugged off her boots and socks as if she were a small child.

Ellie craved a hot bath and peace but would get neither. Her father had recently replaced their bathtub with a new shower, and peace was always in short supply in the Teague house. She had no right to complain, though, because she was sure her parents hadn't expected their two grown children to end up living at home again. Ellie had moved out of the flat she'd shared with her friend Patsy in the run-up to her wedding and simply stayed on after everything fell apart. Meanwhile her brother, his wife and their new baby were all crammed into Grant's childhood bedroom while they waited for their new house to be built. To say that it was overcrowded and chaotic was an understatement.

'I'm going up to shower, Mum, before I freeze to death.'

'You do that. Bring your wet clothes down when you're done and I'll get them washed.'

Ellie purposely didn't mention her meeting with Liam because her mother would tell her what rumours were floating around the village about the intriguing stranger, and for now she wanted to keep him to herself.

After she finished her shower, Ellie towelled herself dry and slathered her skin with her favourite rose-scented lotion. She pulled on hot-pink sweatpants and a thick purple jumper before adding purple socks and her fluffy yellow bunny slippers. A quick glance in the mirror made her smile, thinking of sophisticated, well-dressed Will's reaction if he could see her now.

You're done with him. Let it go.

'Ellie, your tea's ready.'

She angrily brushed away a rogue tear. 'I'll be right there, Mum.'

★　★　★

The charcoal flew over the paper, and within minutes Liam held Ellie's likeness in his hands. He stuck the drawing on the corkboard in the kitchen and stood back, analysing it critically. A flicker of satisfaction darted through him, because even without the addition of colour he'd captured her vibrancy and natural unadorned beauty. Maybe his theatrical agent was right. *Try a change of scenery*, he'd said. *What've you got to lose? We all want the old Liam back.*

Nobody seemed to understand there was no 'old Liam' left. Did Randy Lecroix seriously think that putting an ocean between Liam and his memories would wash them away?

He ripped down the drawing, screwed it into a ball and tossed it in the bin.

Trelanow is a small village. You'll have to work hard to avoid me. Ellie's words echoed in his head. Avoidance was his specialty these days.

2

'Come on, Ellie, don't be boring.' Patsy pleaded. 'Let's show the men around here what they're missing.'

'Karaoke night at the Red Lion, seriously?'

'We don't need to sing. In fact, in your case it's banned.' She laughed. 'It'll be fun, and neither of us have had much of that recently.'

The pointed comment struck home. Patsy had lost her hairdressing job months ago when the salon went out of business and had only managed to pick up some part-time work in the local Co-op. Her lack of income, combined with losing Ellie's rent money, meant she'd been forced to give up the flat they'd shared. Patsy had moved back home to help out her widowed father, who'd taken early retirement from his building job and was waiting to have both knees replaced.

'Saturday is two-for-one fish and chips night, so it won't cost much.' Patsy grinned. 'Maybe if I'm lucky Harry will be there.'

'Harry Richards? Why would that make any difference?' Ellie's questions made her old friend frown. 'Did I just put my foot in it? I didn't realise you were interested in him.'

'He's got a nice smile and . . . he's kind, Ellie, and decent. Isn't that worth something?'

'Of course it is. But do you fancy him?'

'I think I might.' Patsy's cheeks burned. 'Be a friend and come with me.'

What a choice. A grim karaoke night at the local pub, or watching *Strictly* with her parents while baby Marc screamed and his desperate parents struggled to get him to sleep. 'All right,' she sighed. 'Meet you there at seven?'

'Perfect.' Patsy eyed her up and down. 'I'd suggest you get rid of the bunny slippers before then.'

'I was dressed for a night in,' Ellie protested.

'Slap on some make-up. No trousers for once. Skirt and heels.' She tugged Ellie's plait. 'Get rid of this; it's too school-teachery.'

'I *am* a school teacher. Are there any more orders while you're at it?'

'No.' Patsy touched her arm. 'I know it's hard to get back out there. I wanted to crawl under a rock after Dev and I broke up.'

The four of them had started school together aged five — Patsy, Ellie, Dev and Will. Inseparable all the way through to secondary school, they'd paired off in their teens and often gone on double dates. The first crack in their close bond came when Will, the cleverest of the group, went to Oxford before becoming a high-powered lawyer in London. Ellie had gone off to Exeter to train as a primary school teacher and then returned to live in Trelanow while working in nearby St. Austell. Patsy and

Dev never left the village, and everyone assumed they would marry young and soon have a house full of babies. But Dev had strung Patsy along, then shocked everyone last year by dumping her and turning right around to marry a girl he met on holiday in France.

Ellie plastered on a smile. 'I'd better get ready.'

'Thanks.' Patsy hugged her. 'You're the best. I'll see you later.'

Ellie didn't move straight away.

Her mother bustled into the kitchen and set their dirty coffee mugs in the sink. 'Your father thought he heard Patsy's voice. Did she want anything in particular?'

A suspicion trickled into Ellie's head. 'Why don't you tell me?' Her mother's cheeks burned. 'Is it 'get sad Ellie out of the house' night?'

'Don't be cross, love. We're worried about you, and so is Patsy.'

Ellie took a couple of steadying breaths. Her parents had been wonderful, never condemning her for walking out on an expensive wedding or complaining about her continuing presence at home. 'I appreciate that, but I don't need my social life kick-started, no matter how well-meaning you all might be. I'll go tonight because I won't let Patsy down, but please don't plan anything like this again.'

'You never know; you might enjoy yourself.'

'Stop while you're ahead, Mum.' She shook her head and left with her mother's gentle laughter ringing in her ears.

★   ★   ★

Liam couldn't stand being alone in the quiet cottage any longer, and his rumbling stomach reminded him he hadn't eaten all day. He dragged on his old black coat and smiled at the notion of the worn-out garment gaining Ellie's approval. He'd take a walk into the village to find a decent pub and hope that being around other people might encourage him to eat. The last doctor he saw lectured him on taking better care of himself and not jeopardising his recovery from the accident that had taken Cathy's life. He'd almost asked whether it really mattered.

The clear moonlit night surprised him when he stepped out of the door because he'd assumed it would still be raining. He pulled on his wool hat and took care to lock the door and leave the outside light ready on for his return. He'd grown curiously attached to the cottage over the last week with its quirky oddly shaped rooms, plain whitewashed walls, and mismatched furniture. The large glossy apartment he'd left behind in New York seemed a lifetime away.

He strolled down the narrow street and couldn't resist sneaking a glimpse into the houses he walked past. An old lady sat alone at her kitchen table, her rounded shoulders and slumped body indicating profound sadness. In another, a couple slumped in their armchairs in a darkened room and stared at a flickering television screen. Two young boys fighting over a toy car were being pulled apart by their irate mother. He'd take a guess that bed time couldn't come soon enough for her.

Liam turned the corner and spotted several people entering the Red Lion pub. A sudden urge to return to the cottage gripped him, but then a sudden blast of music and laughing voices drifted out onto the pavement, luring him closer. A flyer in the window read: 'Saturday Special! Karaoke night and two-for-one fish and chips.'

'You goin' in, mate?'

Liam apologised for blocking the door and stepped inside, hit by a blast of welcome warmth. He managed to make his way through the packed room to the bar and pulled off his woolly hat, shaking out his hair.

The barman slapped a beer mat down in front of Liam. 'What're you having?'

'No idea. You got any recommendations?'

'You must be the Yank staying in Pascoe's old cottage.'

Liam wasn't about to go into the ins and outs of not calling someone from the south a Yank.

'Try a pint of Doom Bar. It's local and good beer.'

'That'll do.'

'Fish and chips?'

At that exact moment a waitress walked by carrying a couple of steaming platefuls of food, and the tempting aroma made his mouth water. 'Yeah, why not.'

'There's a few tables left if you want, or you can stay and eat up here.'

Liam glanced around and his gaze rested on two women chattering in the far corner with wine glasses in their hands. He'd been right on the beach: Ellie's hair deserved to be let loose. The bright pub lighting picked up the touch of red he'd missed before, and the shimmering mass of waves skimmed the thin straps of her eye-catching turquoise dress.

'You made up your mind?' the barman asked. He put a glass under the pump and filled it slowly, letting it settle before topping it off and setting it in front of Liam.

'Sorry. Here's fine.' He didn't want to draw attention to himself, and walking around to look for a table would do precisely that. Liam took a cautious sip of his beer. 'You were right. It's good.'

'Your food won't be long. The karaoke starts at eight if you're interested.'

'Doubtful.'

The barman grinned. 'Didn't think so. Not my thing either, but it pulls the punters in.' He gave Liam a shrewd stare. 'By the way, I'm Matt. Matt Brewer. And yes, I've heard every joke a million times before. My dad owns this place and we're fourth-generation inn-keepers.' He chuckled. 'Beer's in our blood.'

'I can't talk, not with a name like Liam Delaroche. That's what you get when you mix an Irish mother with a Creole father.'

'You staying here long?'

'I'm not sure yet.'

'I'd better get busy or Dad will skin

me.' Matt's barman's intuition had kicked in. The best always knew who wanted to continue a conversation and who didn't.

Liam returned to his beer and sneaked a quick glance over his shoulder at Ellie. A big ruddy-faced man with glasses and a thick black beard had joined her table, but by the way he leaned closer to Ellie's dark-haired friend, that was where his interest lay. Not that it concerned Liam one way or the other. *Yeah, right, who are you fooling?* The normal, friendly thing to do would be to stroll over and say hello, but the idea of talking to Ellie in front of other people kept him fixed to the bar stool.

All of a sudden she caught him staring and her mouth gaped open.

3

'Who's the vampire?' Patsy asked.

Ellie dragged her gaze away from Liam. 'What on earth are you talking about?'

'The dark, mysterious man propping up the bar, dressed like a gravedigger and looking as though he hasn't seen daylight in a year. I suspect he's trying to decide if you'd make a tasty meal.' Patsy laughed and licked her lips in an exaggerated fashion.

'You're being ridiculous. He's a little pale, that's all.'

'Pale? I've seen white sheets with more colour.' A smirk crept over her face. 'You know him, don't you?' When Ellie didn't respond, her friend turned towards Harry. 'Have you seen Mr. Creepy before?'

'No.' Harry shrugged. 'I suppose he's a visitor.'

Patsy switched her attention back to Ellie. 'If you don't tell me, I'll go up and ask him to come and join us.'

'You ... ' She'd been about to say 'you wouldn't', but her extraverted friend wouldn't hesitate to follow through on her threat. 'We bumped into each other on the beach this afternoon, that's all.'

'What's his name? Where's he from?'

'Is this twenty questions?'

'Ellie Teague, stop wriggling. I'll find out sooner or later.' Patsy wagged her middle finger.

Ellie gave in. 'We only spoke for a couple of minutes. He's the American who's renting Mrs Pascoe's old cottage and his name's Liam Delaroche.' *His intense grey eyes turn to silver when he smiles, and you should hear him talk. Butter dripping off hot toast comes to mind.*

'What's he doing here?'

'By the look of things, I'd say he's having a drink and eating fish and chips, the same as us.' Ellie's pert reply earned her a snort.

'I meant in Trelanow. Don't try to be clever. It doesn't suit you.'

'I don't know why he's here, Patsy.' Ellie couldn't hide her exasperation. 'We spoke for all of five minutes. I didn't know I'd be grilled about our conversation or I'd have asked him for a detailed biography.'

'You fancy him, don't you?' Patsy stared towards the bar. 'He's the total opposite of Will, I'll grant you that. If you're attracted to dark, lean and brooding, he ticks all the boxes.'

'I never said — '

'You don't need to. Your face says it all.' Patsy laughed. 'You seem to forget I've known you since you were five. I knew you had a crush on Bobby Green before you did.'

'For heaven's sake, leave her alone,' Harry pleaded.

'I only . . . ' Patsy went quiet and subsided back in her chair.

Seeing her friend take notice of the soft-spoken older man amused Ellie.

She knew very little about Harry apart from the fact that he lived with his widowed mother, worked in a local bank, and ran the church choir.

'I'll get the next round.' Ellie jumped up and grabbed their empty glasses. She refused to be a coward. Being polite to a stranger was no big deal.

'Good luck.'

She ignored Patsy's sly dig and eased her way around the closely packed tables. At the bar she caught Matt's eye. 'Same again please.'

'Isn't one of us supposed to say 'fancy seeing you here'?' Liam joked.

'If you remember, I told you it'd be hard to avoid me.'

Liam's dark eyes swept over Ellie, setting her pulse racing. 'I haven't forgotten anything about you.'

'Weren't the fish and chips any good?' She pointed to his barely touched plate of food.

'I wasn't as hungry as I thought. And yeah, I know I ought to eat it, but . . . ' His voice trailed away.

'Why don't you come over and join us? It's not much fun eating alone.'

'I couldn't possibly.'

'Why not?' Ellie persisted. 'I'm only here with a couple of my friends, and they'd like to meet you.'

'So your girlfriend can try to find out what she couldn't manage from you?' Liam's soft chuckle took her aback.

'Patsy can be nosey, but she's a good friend. The best.'

'I'm sure. You're lucky.' Liam gestured all around them. 'Don't take any of this for granted.'

She wasn't certain how to respond.

'Sorry, I'm being weird tonight.'

Only tonight?

'That's not kind.' His unexpected broad smile stripped away a layer of the apartness surrounding him.

'Do you need a tray, Ellie?'

She'd forgotten all about their drinks. 'Yes please, Matt.' Taking a chance, she repeated her offer to Liam. 'Come on. Bring your plate. Our food will be here in a minute.'

He couldn't turn down Ellie's challenge. As an artist he could stare at her all day, trying to work out how best to express her gentle beauty in his work; but as a man he was bewildered at the way she'd kindled something he'd thought was dead inside him. It went beyond physical attraction to a yearning to dig deeper and learn more about her.

'You win.' Liam eased off the stool. 'Lead the way.' He juggled a fresh pint in one hand and his plate in the other.

'Grab another chair, Harry.' Ellie set the tray down on the table and introduced Liam.

'It's good to meet you. I'm Patsy Watkins. If you want to hear any dirt on this one, just say.' She tapped Ellie's arm, 'I know it all.'

'I might take you up on that.'

'Ignore her,' Ellie snapped. 'Here's our food.' The waitress appeared, balancing three plates. 'Sit down, Liam, and eat.'

'Yes, ma'am.' He couldn't help smiling again; she kept doing that to him. 'You aren't a teacher by any chance, are you?'

'Aren't you the sharp one? I'm surprised you don't cut yourself.'

'Did I hit the nail on the head?' Liam chuckled. 'Let me guess. Little ones.' He could picture her mothering kindergarten children in a firm, loving way. 'I'll eat, I promise. Would you like me to write out one hundred times 'I must not be rude to the teacher' first?'

The corners of her mouth twitched with amusement, and another knot of tension inside Liam unravelled. 'You're impossible,' Ellie griped halfheartedly.

He picked up his fork and stabbed a bite of fish, shoving it into his mouth. 'Eat up. Yours is getting cold.'

'Now who's giving orders?'

'Are you two going to stop bickering?' Patsy asked. 'Some of us were hoping for a pleasant evening out.'

'I'm having one anyway,' Harry declared. 'This is a whole lot better than watching that stupid dancing programme with my mother. Talk about a load of old codswallop.'

'A load of what?' Liam laid down his fork. 'I'm guessing that's another Briticism I haven't heard before.' The other man's ruddy skin went bright red. 'Sorry, I didn't mean to embarrass you. I'm interested, that's all. We're supposed to all speak English, but that's up for debate I'd say.'

'If you're really interested, the story goes that there was a British soft-drink maker named Codd and beer lovers made up the sarcastic name for his product using the word 'wallop', which is a slang term for beer.' Ellie rattled off the detailed explanation and he openly stared at her.

'She's a word nut,' Patsy said. 'Ellie's always been a bit weird.'

'I'm into etymology, that's all, and in particular folk etymology. I love finding out where our common words and expressions come from.'

'Hey, you don't have to defend yourself. It's fascinating.' Liam grasped her hand. 'Let's eat.'

'Um, I need my hand back.'

'Okay. If you must.' What made him say that? The little nibble she gave her lip. The tinge of colour highlighting her cheekbones. The way she awkwardly pushed a lock of hair back from her face. He squeezed her warm fingers before letting go.

Patsy changed the conversation and talked about a concert Harry's choir was giving next week for Easter Sunday.

'You see, I was right.' Ellie pointed to Liam's plate, and he discovered he'd finished the mound of fish and chips while they were all talking. All of a sudden she froze, lost all of her colour and shrank back into herself.

'What's wrong?' When she didn't answer, Liam draped his arm around her shoulder, pulling her close.

'Oh wonderful, just what we don't need,' Patsy muttered and stared over at the door.

4

Ellie considered crawling under the table but wouldn't give Will the satisfaction. She couldn't blame him for exacting a measure of revenge by walking into their local pub with his arm around a glamorous redhead, but it felt as if she'd been kicked in the stomach. Of course Will always did enjoy being the centre of attention, and his broad smile said he was loving every minute of this.

'Keep breathing nice and steady,' Liam whispered.

'Hello, Ellie. Long time no see.' Will's drawl, affected to wipe out his Cornish accent, made her wince. 'Patsy. Harry. Good to see you both.' He beamed at the woman glued to his side. 'This is Lavinia Goodall. We came down from London for the weekend.'

Ellie fixed a fake smile in place when Will introduced them all to his companion, and barely managed to hold onto it when he included Ellie under the heading of 'old friend'.

'And you are?' Will gave Liam a searching stare.

'Liam Delaroche. New 'friend'.'

'Of course.' His snide tone annoyed Ellie. 'Makes sense now.'

'We're not . . . ' She stopped right there. Getting into a slanging match in the middle of the pub wasn't a good idea. 'Enjoy your evening, and say hello to your parents from me. I hope they're keeping well.'

'Thank you, they are. And yours?'

'Fine, thank you.' Ellie stifled a giggle. They sounded like a couple from a Jane Austen novel making polite conversation at a ball.

'Are we staying *here* for the evening?' Lavinia sneered and glanced around the packed bar.

'We don't have to, sweetheart,' Will assured her, and Ellie's annoyance grew. The Red Lion was perfectly good enough when *they'd* been a couple, but clearly didn't rate for her replacement.

'You aren't going to stay and show off your karaoke skills?' Liam asked.

'Hardly,' Will scoffed. 'That was never Ellie's thing either in the old days, but maybe she's changed. I'd say for the better. We love it, don't we, honey?' He squeezed Lavinia's shoulder, and Ellie managed another forced smile.

'Oh, we certainly do,' Lavinia gushed.

'Maybe we'll stay awhile after all. I have to hear this. I can only assume Ellie's been taking singing lessons.'

For two pins, Ellie silently declared she'd smack Will's smug face. He knew she couldn't hold a tune to save her life and even had to mouth the words to Christmas carols.

'You might be surprised,' Liam said. What was he playing at?

Will's eyes narrowed. The challenge wasn't lost on him or anybody else, judging by Patsy's and Harry's frowns. 'Why don't you find us a table while I get the drinks?' he suggested to Lavinia.

'A table?'

'Yes,' he snapped, and turned back to Ellie. 'Good luck.'

'Thanks very much, but we don't need it.' She flashed a brilliant smile at Liam. 'He's an amazing partner . . . singing partner, that is.'

'You're pretty damn good yourself.' Liam pressed a soft kiss on her cheek, and the fleeting brush of his lips made Ellie's cheeks flame.

Oh no I'm not. You have no idea.

As Will drew Lavinia away, Ellie swung around to face Liam. 'Are you out of your tiny little mind?'

'Yes he is,' Patsy laughed. 'He doesn't know the words 'tone-deaf' and 'caterwauling' were created with my dearest friend in mind.'

All of the superiority seeping through Will Burton's every word and gesture had stirred Liam up. But now a trickle of common sense crept back into his brain. For someone trying not to draw attention to himself, he'd done the worst possible thing. 'He riled me,' he explained. 'I'm sorry. We can bail. It won't bother me.'

'Well it'd bother *me*,' Ellie declared. 'I'll do it if it kills me.'

'It's the poor souls who'll be listening that I feel sorry for,' Patsy chimed in.

'I've got an idea,' Harry ventured. 'How about we do a foursome? Patsy can carry a tune, and I'll take a guess you can too, Liam?'

'Yeah.' That was a wild understatement, but he couldn't go into details without raising more questions.

'Good,' Harry said. 'We'll sing loud, and all Ellie needs to do is mouth the words.'

'It won't work, because she won't be able to resist joining in,' Patsy chided. 'She always thinks it'll be different.'

Ellie contented herself with glowering at her friend.

'She knows I'm right.'

'Don't fret,' Liam said, trying to keep the peace. 'We'll pull it off. How about we try *Summer Nights* from *Grease*?'

Harry frowned. 'I suppose it's as good

as anything. Ellie, you stick to very quietly helping out with the chorus. Patsy, you'll have to do Olivia Newton-John's part.' He glanced at Liam. 'You'd better take the lead. I'm more of a bass. Not exactly John Travolta material.'

'I appreciate you all doing this for me,' Ellie mumbled.

'I'll go up and put our names down.' Harry disappeared towards the bar.

'I'll explain about Will later.' Ellie's small worried voice tugged at Liam. 'It's complicated.' Her head rested against his shoulder, and Liam couldn't resist running his fingers through her thick springy hair. His touch released the intoxicating scent of wildflowers and made him want things he shouldn't.

'You don't have to,' he said.

'Yes, I do.' The hint of steel he'd picked up on at the beach had returned and he wasn't stupid enough to argue.

'We're up first.' Harry's announcement silenced them all. 'I thought we might as well get it over with.'

'The sooner the better.' Ellie grimaced.

'If nothing else, it'll get rid of Will and his 'I'm too good for an ordinary pub' girlfriend.'

'Let's get the karaoke underway,' Matt yelled over the crowd. 'Give a big Red Lion hand to our first brave souls. They call themselves the Four Musketeers, so let's hear it for our very own Ellie, Patsy, and Harry, joined tonight by their transatlantic friend Liam.'

'Come on. We'll show them.' Liam's assurance garnered a wry smile from Ellie. He led the way over to the tiny stage and picked up one of the microphones. It'd been a long time since he'd performed without doing his vocal exercises, extensive practising and a sound check of the venue, but the familiar knot of nerves tightened in the pit of his stomach. 'Ready, everyone?'

Ellie's fear showed in her pale, strained face and he wished he could beg her to trust him to get her through this. The music started and Liam focused on Patsy, the supposed Sandy to his Danny. He kept his eyes half-closed and pretended to be singing to Ellie.

His voice soared into the room as the music swept him away. Patsy's tentative efforts made him pay closer attention, and he gave her an encouraging smile. In the background Harry took the lead on the chorus, and his strong deep voice almost succeeded in swamping Ellie's tuneless attempts to keep up. Liam slipped into performance mode and played to the crowd, getting them to sing along. By the time they finished, he carelessly wiped away the sweat trickling down his face.

'Great job,' Matt proclaimed. 'I wouldn't like to be next is all I can say.'

Liam met Ellie's curious stare. Back at their table, nobody spoke for a minute until Harry offered to get the drinks in.

'Carry a tune, can you, Liam Delaroche?' Ellie's pointed question made him squirm. 'I'm not the only one with some explaining to do.'

Patsy blushed and whispered something to Ellie, who instantly turned to him. 'Can you do me one more favour, or rather my hopeless friend here?'

'Sure. What do you need?'

'Could you drink up quickly and then say that we're leaving? Make it sound to Harry as though you can't wait to get me on your own.'

That won't be a hardship, he thought.

'Ask Harry to make sure Patsy gets home all right.' Ellie lowered her voice. 'He's shy, and if she doesn't make the first move they'll never get anywhere.'

Liam suppressed a smile. So this was how women got what they wanted where men were concerned. 'I can manage that.' He made sure he couldn't be overheard and whispered in her ear, 'On one condition — I get a good-night kiss in return.' He almost backed out and retracted his request, but Ellie's shy smile stopped him. *Keep looking at me that way. Please.*

'I don't see why not.'

I do, honey, a thousand times over. But I don't want you to — not yet.

5

Ellie had never seen any man look so ridiculously pleased at the prospect of kissing her. She hated to spoil the moment and warn him it would probably be a major disappointment.

Harry arrived with their drinks. 'Here we go. I'd like to propose a toast to Pavarotti here.' He tilted his glass in Liam's direction. 'Will you still be around next week?'

'Probably. Why?'

'The church choir could do with you for the special music we're singing for the Easter service.'

Ellie caught Patsy's admiring gaze and wondered how long her friend had harboured a secret crush on Harry.

'I'm sure if you agreed we'd see a surge of interest, especially among the women, after tonight's performance. This will be all around the village by morning.'

'I thought a young John Travolta had popped unnoticed into the Red Lion when you belted that one out,' Patsy teased.

'You weren't so bad yourself,' Liam muttered, and Ellie sensed his awkwardness.

'You carried me and made me look good. Maybe they'll want me in the choir now too if I play my cards right.'

Harry's cheeks glowed. 'Of course you'd be welcome. I never thought to ask before. You never — '

'I'm pulling your leg.'

'I'm not.'

Ellie was startled as Liam squeezed her hand. 'Are we still on for that walk?' he asked, and gave Harry an apologetic nod. 'I'm sorry to break up the party, but Ellie promised to be my tour guide for the highlights of Trelanow at night time.'

'That should take you all of ten minutes if she really drags it out,' Patsy teased.

'You'll see Patsy home won't you,

Harry?' Ellie said.

'Uh, yes, of course.'

Ellie tried not to laugh at his bemused disbelief. He plainly couldn't believe his luck.

'Let's go.' Liam took her by surprise and jerked them both to their feet before sweeping her into a tight hug. 'They're watching us, so I'll make it good,' he whispered, and touched his mouth to hers before she could ask what he meant.

Over his shoulder, Ellie caught Will and Lavinia staring at them, but then everything in the room disappeared except Liam's clean, warm scent surrounding her. He shoved his hands up through her hair and gave a gentle tug to pull her closer. Far too soon he eased away, ending the kiss.

'That should do the trick.' Liam's silvery eyes gleamed, and without another word he grasped hold of her hand and led her out through the bar. They stepped out of the pub and the chill night air hit Ellie, making her shiver.

'It's okay, honey. I won't get the

wrong impression and read too much into this. If you prefer, I'll walk you straight home.'

Ellie took several slow, deep breaths. Liam's offer made sense, but his draw over her wouldn't loosen. She linked her arm through his. 'While we walk, you can tell me why you floored everyone back there in the pub? And in return I'll explain about me and Will.' His jaw line tightened, and she wondered if she was pushing him too far. 'Do we have a deal?'

Why couldn't he say no to her?

'I don't have any thumbscrews.' She waved her hands in the air and grinned. The soft moonlight illuminated her from the inside out and took Liam's breath away. He was sure she'd scoff if he called her beautiful. She'd insist her figure was too curvy, say that freckles were unfashionable and bemoan her thick, undisciplined hair.

You don't need thumbscrews. I'm already lost.

'If you want. It's nothing startling.'

Liam shrugged. 'Let's walk.' Without over-thinking it, he took hold of her small warm hand. 'Which way?'

'Over to the right. We'll head towards the far side of the quay. There's a bench where we can sit and be sheltered from the wind.'

He slowed his usual fast pace to match her shorter stride. 'Have the Teagues lived here forever? I always imagine in places like this the families are all intermingled and everyone you meet is related in some way.'

'That sounds a bit creepy,' Ellie laughed, 'but I suppose you're right. There have been Teagues in Trelanow since the late seventeen hundreds.' She stopped walking and stared up at him, her face solemn and lovelier than ever. 'I thought I could leave it, but in the end . . . '

'I'm guessin' a lot more was wrong with the scenario apart from geography.'

'Right again.' Her attempt at a smile didn't reach her eyes. 'Let's keep going.

It's too chilly to stand still for long.'

Liam mentally kicked himself for not realising Ellie's linen jacket was no protection against the bitter wind. 'It makes a change for me to be the sensibly dressed one tonight. Take this.' Liam ignored her protests and draped his heavy wool coat around her shoulders. 'Better?'

'It's still warm from you.' He caught a seductive hint of her blush in the moonlight. 'Thanks.'

For a few minutes they walked along without speaking, both wrapped in their own thoughts.

'Here we go.' The old wood bench was nestled in the cliff side and protected by a jagged granite overhang. Liam had no doubt that more than a few courting couples favoured this spot, he sat down next to Ellie and waited.

'If you listened to any village gossip, you'd already have heard about my scandalous behaviour. In November I left Will standing at the altar. It wasn't my finest hour.'

'I've only been here a week and haven't ventured out much.'

'Will is the local golden boy from another old Trelanow family. Some people think he's a bit uppity these days, but mostly they forgive him because he's a successful barrister up in London and does right by his mum and dad.'

Liam held his tongue. The other man's manner tonight hadn't implied much in the way of affection for either the village or his family.

'We'd been friends since we started primary school,' Ellie continued. 'We started going out together when we were teenagers, and getting married was the next logical step in everyone's eyes. Very few people could understand why I'd turn down the chance to get away and 'make something of myself'.'

''Yourself' looks like a pretty good thing from where I am.'

She threw him a sharp glance. 'What do you know? You only met me . . . ' Ellie peered at the illuminated dial on

44

her watch. ' . . . six hours ago.'

'I'm pretty sure you love your job and the children in your class.'

'Yes, of course I do.'

'And you've got a good, close family, right? They probably annoy you at times, but I'll bet anything they're always there for you.'

Ellie nodded. 'So?'

'You've got so much and don't even realise it.' He fought to keep the envy out of his voice.

'You don't have those things?'

I did but I let them go.

'Sorry. Am I not supposed to ask? I thought we made a deal.' Ellie's eyes flared in an unmistakeable challenge.

'Yeah, we did.' Liam picked up her cold hands. 'I had an amazing supportive family and a stellar career as a Broadway artist.'

'That explains the singing.'

'I could've done the full John Travolta dance routine if I'd wanted to show off.'

'So what happened?'

'I messed up. Trust me, you leaving Mr. Wonderful at the altar is child's play compared to what I managed to achieve.'

'We all make mistakes. I'm pretty certain no one died from yours.'

'Why?'

'Why what?' Liam let go of her and stood up. 'The six-hours rule applies both ways. I'll walk you home.'

'What did I say?' Ellie pleaded, and a heartbeat of agonising silence hung between them. Quietly she rose from the bench to join him. 'Who died, Liam?'

Her whispered question tore at his heart and Clare's name stuck in his throat.

'I'm terribly sorry.' She leaned her head against his chest, and the gesture made it impossible for him to resist wrapping his arms around her. He clung to her as if she were a lifebelt thrown to a drowning man. 'You obviously forgot I'm nosey and not in the least bit tactful.'

'I won't forget again.' He struggled to match her forlorn effort to lighten the moment. 'Home?'

'Probably for the best.'

Sometimes there really was nothing more to say. It'd been crazy to come here in the first place. Tomorrow he'd pack his bags and draw a line under his failed expedition to Cornwall. Liam loosened his grasp on Ellie and gently took hold of her hand instead, unable to resist the chance to touch her one last time.

6

We all make mistakes. I'm pretty certain no one died from yours.

Ellie's careless words haunted her all night, and as the first flickers of dawn crept into the room she abandoned the idea of sleep. Turning on her bedside light, she tossed back the covers and grabbed an old jumper from the chair to drag on over her nightdress. She picked her way around the creaky floorboards and sat down at the dressing table. She opened her laptop and her finger hovered over the power button. What would she do if she discovered something she'd rather not know and that Liam definitely hadn't wanted to tell her?

She quietly closed the lid and rested her hands on top. Despite Liam's gaunt appearance, there was an inherently masculine grace about him when he moved, and after hearing him sing she could totally picture him performing on stage. He'd command a Broadway audience in the same way he'd held everyone in the pub in the palm of his hand.

Ellie touched a finger to her lips where Liam's warm fleeting kiss lingered in her memory. After unconsciously putting her foot in it last night, she didn't expect him to seek her out again anytime soon. Maybe this afternoon she'd give Grant and Tina a break and offer to take the baby for a walk. If they happened to go in the direction of Jetty Street and wandered past Mrs. Pascoe's cottage — it was a free country, wasn't it?

'Are you up?' her mum whispered outside the door.

'Yes, Mum.'

'Thought you must be. I spotted your light. I've brought you some tea.'

'What've I done to deserve this?' she joked as she opened the door and held out her hand to take the steaming mug.

'Did you have a nice time last night?'

It wasn't hard to guess that a little bird called Patsy had been talking — or maybe *singing* was more appropriate. 'Come in.' The fascinating story of their karaoke efforts, Will and his new girl-friend turning up at the pub, and her own disappearing act afterwards with the unknown American was doubtless all around the village by now. 'What did you hear?'

Jennifer bristled. 'Why would I have heard *anything*? You're a grown woman, and I've got better things to do with my time than check up on you.'

No one could flip Ellie's guilt switch as well as her dear mother. 'Of course you do.' She calmly ran through the bare bones of the evening, skimming over her run-in with Will and avoiding all mention of Liam's very public kiss.

'How did Will seem?'

Smug. Self-satisfied. Like a stranger. 'The same. The woman with him is his new type. Glossy and brittle. Too good for here.' Ellie's casual dismissal of her ex earned her a frown. 'It didn't bother me to see him again, if that's what you're worried about.' That was the absolute truth, and maybe a touch sad after all the years they'd been together. 'Honestly.'

'Good.' Jennifer cleared her throat. 'You know, I'm glad you didn't go through with the wedding.'

'Really?'

'I should've said so before.' The colour rose in her cheeks. 'I was too bustled up about cancelling the reception and returning all of the presents.'

Ellie set her mug down on top of the dresser. 'You and Dad were wonderful. You could've been cross at me for wasting all that money and embarrassing everyone.'

'All we ever wanted was for you to be happy. Nothing else mattered.'

Ellie nodded and blinked away a rush of tears.

'But I must admit, I did hear you've got a new admirer who's a bit of a singer.'

'Patsy's exaggerating.'

'She only said . . . ' Jennifer slapped a hand over her mouth and laughed. 'Oops.'

'It doesn't matter. If a strange man kisses me in the middle of the Red Lion, I can hardly expect to keep it quiet.'

'True. When do we get to meet the mystery man?'

'For goodness sake, Mum, I only met him yesterday.' *And I doubt we're even speaking today.* 'Thanks for the tea. I'm going to have a quick shower, and then I'll come down and make breakfast for everyone.'

'In other words, stop being nosey.'

Ellie merely smiled. Living at home again was a delicate balancing act for them all.

'I'll expect the full works — bacon, sausages, eggs, tomatoes and fried bread at the very least.' Jennifer wagged her finger. 'Plus you can do the dishes afterwards.'

'Deal.' Ellie struggled to keep breathing as the memory slammed back: *Do we have a deal?* 'I'll see you in a few minutes.'

* * *

Abandoned drawings littered the kitchen table and spilled onto the floor. Liam had worked feverishly all night, and was now fighting to keep his eyes open long enough to finish the picture in front of him. Before the accident he'd developed a passion for charcoal drawing, and had considered a career change in that direction when he'd had enough of performing. He loved the stripped-down aspect of this particular medium, where the only colour came from the subtle shading of dark versus light. Very much like life.

Ellie's enigmatic smile taunted him, and he rested his fingers on her beautiful face. If only he could've been honest with her last night, things might have been different, but at the last second he'd drawn back.

His head throbbed with a combination

of sleeplessness and hunger. There was nothing here to eat, so he could wander down to the pub in search of food. Matt might be behind the bar again, and perhaps a little normal conversation would fix what ailed him.

Liam heaved himself out of the chair and trudged up the narrow stairs. He took a long enough shower for the pitiful water supply to run cold, then dressed in his only remaining clean clothes. The only concession he made to his appearance was in raking a comb through his long straggly hair.

A loud banging noise interrupted his thoughts and Liam peered out of the window. He backed out of sight when he saw Ellie standing outside his door with a baby in a stroller. She knocked again but he stayed where he was until he heard her leave. A couple of minutes later he crept downstairs and saw a scrap of paper on the doormat. Liam picked up the handwritten note and sighed.

I'll be down on the quay if you fancy

some fresh air. I've got my nephew with me, so feel free to stay away if you're allergic to babies! Ellie.

Liam unhitched his coat from the hook by the door and slipped it on before he hurried out into the street. As he turned the corner, the blustery wind whipped his hair around his face.

'Hey, watch out, mate. We don't want our star karaoke act blown into the sea.' Matt laughed, putting out a hand to steady him. 'You were the talk of the place last night. Everyone's hoping you'll come again next Saturday; liven things up a bit.'

Liam struggled to be polite. 'I only sang to please . . . a friend.'

'I'll tell you straight. More than a few folks were happy to see Will Burton's nose put out of joint.'

'Worked for me.' Liam grinned.

'Of course, others weren't pleased to see you hitched up with Ellie. Several men have been biding their time before making a move.'

'Whoa — you're jumping to the

wrong conclusion,' he protested.

'I don't think so.' Matt shook his head. 'If you two had sparked any more electricity last night, you'd have blown all the fuses. Don't worry; your secret's safe with me.' He winked. 'I'll be late for work if I don't get my skates on. See you around.'

'Yeah, see ya,' Liam replied automatically, shaken by Matt's blunt assessment. On stage he laid everything out, with every emotion bare and exposed, but in his regular life he couldn't be more different. Last night he'd mixed the two up.

'If you stand there much longer, you'll fossilise.'

He spun around to face Ellie. 'Are you trying to give me a heart attack again?'

'Don't be such an old grouse. I was getting an ice-cream at the shop and saw you talking to Matt. Don't worry, I couldn't hear what you were saying.'

'That's not what I — '

'You got my note.'

'Yeah.' Liam shivered and pulled up his coat collar, caught unawares by a waft of Ellie's perfume trapped in the wool from last night. 'Isn't it too cold to eat ice-cream?'

'Never.' She laughed and glanced down at the sleeping baby. 'I'm sure Marc would agree if he could speak.'

'No doubt. Do you want to walk for a while so the ice-cream is the only thing frozen?' He felt her scrutiny. 'You're thinking if I wasn't so scrawny I'd stay warmer, but I blame the damp Cornish weather. It seeps through a person.'

'You like putting words into my mouth, don't you?'

The touch of provocation in what she said ... the smudge of pink gloss shining on her lips ... Matt's casual assumption about them. Everything combined to make Liam do something he'd no doubt regret later.

'Nope. This is much better than words.' He lowered his mouth to hers, and somewhere in the back of his mind he waited to be slapped.

7

Off the charts and better than I remember. Somewhere in the maelstrom of emotions Liam's kiss stirred up, Ellie homed in on that fact.

'Matt was right,' he whispered into her cheek, 'he insisted we had enough electricity going on to blow the fuses.'

'Um, in case you were thinking of doing that again, we're being watched.'

'Who by?'

Ellie peeked around his shoulder. 'Mrs. Bodruggen in the bakery is pretending to clean her windows. John Bates is on the way to pick up his daughter from her piano lesson.' A hot blush rushed up her neck. 'But I'll say the top choice is my mother, who's standing outside the post office talking to the vicar.'

'Shoot.'

'That's one way of putting it.'

A thin wail pierced the air and Ellie

jerked out of Liam's arms. Marc, wide awake and red-faced, had saved her from further ignominy. She bent down and sniffed. 'He smells fine and he shouldn't be hungry yet.'

'Would you mind if I picked him up?'

'You?' The shift in Liam's expression from concerned to hurt made Ellie wish she'd thought before speaking. 'Sorry, I didn't mean — '

'We're experts at that, aren't we?'

Ellie unbuckled Marc and lifted out her squirming nephew. She muttered soothing words and changed positions several times but nothing did the trick. Desperate for her mother not to come over and rush to her rescue, she held him out to Liam. 'Work wonders. Please.'

With a faint smile, he took the hysterical baby from her and rewrapped the blanket tightly in around him with the air of someone who'd done this a million times before. He tucked Marc into the crook of his arm, rocked on his feet and started to sing a tender lullaby Ellie didn't recognise. Marc stopped flailing around and gazed up at Liam. His tiny fingers tugged at a strand of Liam's dark hair and he gurgled happily.

'Wow, you certainly have a knack with babies.' Ellie laughed but Liam didn't join in. The heavy sadness she'd noticed when they first met surrounded him again.

Marc's eyes batted open and closed in a losing battle, and with a little sigh he flopped back in Liam's arms and gave up.

'Do you want to put him back in the buggy?'

'Is that what y'all call it?'

'Either that or a pushchair, but push-chair's a bit old-fashioned these days.'

'To me a buggy is the sort of horse-drawn carriage the Amish people use for transport.'

'Who are they?'

'I'd happily explain, but your mother's headed our way.' The crinkled laugh lines around his eyes deepened. 'I expect you'll need to explain why a strange-looking man is holding her precious grandson.'

Ellie didn't think this was the time or place to tell him that 'strange-looking' was a purely objective term. She'd choose 'unconventional and enigmatic' to start with and could come up with a whole lot more. She waved a warning finger at her mother and mouthed at her to be quiet.

Liam nestled Marc back in the buggy, and her nephew stretched and wriggled a couple of times before settling back to sleep.

'You must be the singing American. I've heard *all* about you.'

Ellie cringed. Couldn't her mother be a little more tactful for once?

'Don't believe everything that comes out of a pub on a Saturday night.' Amusement oozed through Liam's deep, rumbling voice. 'Liam Delaroche.' He stuck out his hand. 'It's a pleasure to meet you, ma'am. If I didn't know better, I'd think you were Ellie's sister.'

Ellie tried to be offended but her mother's satisfied smile mollified her. It interested her to see how charming

Liam could be when he put his mind to it.

'You're very good with babies,' Jennifer observed. 'Do you have a family of your own?'

Why not just ask if he's single and available and be done with it? Ellie fumed.

'I've got three younger brothers and . . . a sister, plus a whole bunch of nieces and nephews. I've done a lot of babysitting in my time.' His smooth reply skimmed over giving Ellie's mother a direct answer but still revealed far more than she'd known a minute ago. 'I ought to be going now.'

'Come home with us for tea.'

'That's very kind of you, but not today.'

'Why not? Do you have something else planned?' Jennifer persisted.

'Mum, don't bug him,' Ellis hissed.

'You're too sensitive. Liam doesn't mind me being friendly. Americans aren't known for being standoffish, are they?'

'No, ma'am, we sure aren't,' Liam

conceded. 'If Ellie doesn't object, I'd be happy to accept.'

'Whyever should she?'

Maybe because it'd be nice to bring someone home when I choose to instead of you having to corner them in the street and dragoon them into coming. 'Mum's Sunday teas are legendary. Come on.'

'Would you like me to push the buggy?' Liam's mouth quirked, and Ellie tried not to laugh at his obvious amusement.

'You might regret making that offer when we're halfway up the hill.' She turned the handle towards him and stood back to let him take over. 'Let's go.'

★ ★ ★

Liam perched on a stool in the corner of the overcrowded room and tried to keep his long legs tucked back out of the way. Ellie's mother a born nurturer, and she'd taken on feeding him as her pet project. He'd been plied with scones served with strawberry jam and something called clotted cream, as well as a huge slice of fruit cake and a selection of small iced cakes bizarrely referred to as fancies.

'Where exactly are you from in America, mate? Ellie didn't say.' Grant's pointed question was no less than he'd expect. Older brothers looked out for their sisters and took care of them if they were worth anything.

'I guess you'd say I'm a bit of a vagabond.' He sensed Ellie listening and stuck with repeating everything he'd told her the day they met.

'So what landed you in Trelanow?'

He'd heard that British people were reticent, but the Teague family plainly didn't go along with the theory. 'An old friend of mine had visited Cornwall and recommended it when I was looking for somewhere quiet to . . . relax. The Pascoes' cottage was advertised on a website I checked out.' None of that was a lie, but it wasn't the complete truth either.

'What's with the singing? You do it professionally?'

'Grant, don't be so nosey,' His wife, Tina, said and blushed. 'Please don't take any notice of my husband. That's the trouble with policemen — they can never leave the job at work.' She playfully prodded his arm.

Liam didn't let his smile falter. A policeman. As soon as he left the house, the other man would check up on him and that would be it.

'It was a straightforward question. Nothing wrong with that, was there?'

'Not at all.' Liam kept his expression blank and worked hard to sound unconcerned. 'I did perform professionally for a long time, mainly in Broadway musicals. I changed direction a couple of years ago, and now I do some voice coaching and a few other things in the artistic sphere.' He deliberately kept his explanations vague.

'How long are you planning to stay in Cornwall?'

'That's enough,' Jennifer scolded. 'I

invited poor Liam here for tea, not to be grilled by you. Ellie isn't sixteen and doesn't need your interference. You don't hear your father sticking his nose in, do you?' She pointed to her husband, who'd barely said a word since Liam arrived.

'He never does,' Grant scoffed. 'He would've let her marry that idiot if she hadn't come to her senses and walked out on him.'

Ellie sprang up from the sofa and planted herself in front of her brother. 'Not that it's any of your business, but Daddy did try to talk me out of it. I stubbornly refused to listen and he very wisely backed off.' She treated her brother to another shrivelling glare. 'You'll find out when Marc's older that you can't run his life for him. At some point you have to sit back, let him make his own mistakes, and be there to pick up the pieces when he needs you.' She brushed away the lone tear trickling down her cheek.

Liam expected Grant to apologise,

but his stony expression didn't change.

'I'll walk back down with you, Liam,' Ellie offered. 'I could do with some fresh air.' Her chin tilted up, and he admired her defiant stance.

'Sure. It's time I was moving anyway.' He eased up off the stool, and everyone gathered around to say goodbye except for Grant. 'You've totally converted me to Sunday tea. It was kind of you to invite me, Mrs. Teague.'

'Please call me Jennifer,' she said, but her fixed smile didn't fool him. Grant would get the sharp side of her tongue later. 'You've seen us at our worst, so you're family now.'

'Yes, ma'am. I'm not sure I can do 'Jennifer' though. It wouldn't be right. I grew up mostly in the south, and the slightly old-fashioned good manners there have stayed with me.' He smiled at Tina, white-faced and plainly embarrassed by her husband's rudeness. 'Anytime you need a babysitter, just let me know.'

'Thanks,' she murmured. 'I hear

you're quite the baby whisperer.'

'Are you ready?' Liam asked Ellie, and her brief nod gave him permission to get them out of there.

Outside the front door, he wrapped his hand around hers but stayed silent. He'd give her the opportunity to choose how much or how little to say. The question really was, how would he answer?

8

'That'll be the last Sunday tea invitation you ever accept.' Ellie attempted to make a joke of it but failed miserably. 'Believe it or not, my brother isn't usually an idiot.'

'He's protective. That's cool.'

'Cool? I don't need him to . . . '

Liam stopped walking and wrapped his arms around her, pulling her into a tight embrace. 'It's okay.' Plastered up against his familiar black coat, Liam's solid warmth soothed her. 'I know you don't 'need' it, but I'm sure he feels guilty.'

'Why?' She couldn't avoid staring into his dark eyes, an intriguing smoky grey in the fading light. 'I make my own choices for good and bad.'

'Oh, honey.' Liam sighed. 'Grant knows that deep down. It doesn't matter if it was your choice to not go through with the wedding. You were still hurt, weren't you?'

Ellie nodded, blinking back tears.

'And he had to stand back and watch you go through that. His frustrations burst through today, that's all.'

'Are you protective with your sister too?'

'Let's keep walking. It's cold.' He let go of her.

'Oh, so you get a glimpse into my messed-up family but I don't get anything in return?'

'It's hard,' he muttered.

'Did you see me having a happy time back there?'

'No.'

'But you still aren't going to answer my question?'

'You don't give up easily, do you?'

'Do you want me to?' Ellie had the nagging sensation that underneath his surface reluctance Liam wanted to talk.

'She's dead. Okay?'

'Oh Liam, I'm so sorry.' Ellie touched his arm but he jerked away.

'Why didn't you say so?'

'Because I don't either want or deserve your sympathy,' he snapped. 'Why don't you run along home? I don't have friends these days, and I'm not in the market for a relationship, so I'd say that about covers it, wouldn't you?'

Ellie recoiled. 'I've got too much pride to stay where I'm not wanted. I hope you enjoy the rest of your stay in Trelanow.' She swung around and hurried back up the hill, wishing her coat was designed with an attached rear-view mirror so she could find out if he was watching her walk away.

* * *

Liam clenched his jaw and refused to call out after her. Two years ago he'd resigned himself to the fact that this was how things would be from now on; but Ellie had touched him in a deep, dark place he'd thought couldn't be breached.

You're no good for her. Leave her

alone. She deserves better. The logical, sensible voice resonated in his head. Grant would soon put Ellie straight about him, and that would put a definite end to whatever this might have been. So why did he have a sick, disappointed knot in his stomach?

Liam shivered and forced himself to keep walking. He made his way down the hill to the harbour and briefly hesitated outside the Red Lion. He wasn't fit company for anyone tonight. Turning the corner into Jetty Street, he came to a sudden halt. He would recognise the stout woman waiting outside his door anywhere.

'I thought I'd have to start scouring the streets for you.'

Liam crossed the road in silence.

'Don't I get a word of welcome?'

'What are *you* doing here?'

'That isn't a very friendly way to talk to your aunt.'

Liam struggled to get his emotions under control. He hadn't spoken to Maria since his sister's funeral, when she'd verbally ripped him to shreds. 'You haven't answered my question.'

'Your parents found out I was coming to London on business and asked me to check on you.' He waited for her to carry on. 'They're worried because they haven't heard from you in ages.'

'How about the truth? We both know you wouldn't travel five miles to visit me out of choice, let alone over three hundred. You made that clear the last time we met — or have you forgotten?'

'No, I sure haven't.' Maria glanced around them at the deserted street. 'Could we go inside? It's cold and I'd rather not talk out here.'

'Fine.' He fished out his keys and unlocked the door. Whatever Maria had come to say, Liam was sure he didn't want to hear it.

* * *

'You're back sooner than I expected.'

Ellie ignored Grant's pointed comment and headed for the stairs.

'Do you want to hear what I found out about your Yank?'

'No, I really don't. I couldn't care less. I won't be seeing him again, so it doesn't matter who or what he is. Are you satisfied now?' Her brother's expression altered. 'Don't.'

'Don't what?'

'Don't you dare feel sorry for me. We're not all lucky enough to have a perfect life.'

'Mine's not — '

'Maybe, but it's a lot closer to it than mine is,' Ellie replied, and then shook her head. 'Forget I said that. You know I love Tina and worship Marc. I didn't mean to sound mean and jealous.'

'Sis, I'm sorry for what I said earlier. I was way out of line.'

She couldn't help smiling. 'Did Tina have a go at you?'

'Understatement,' he muttered under his breath. 'I'll be sleeping on the sofa tonight if I'm not careful.'

'Quite right too,' Ellie quipped.

'Did Liam do something to annoy

you when you left here?'

'I am not discussing him.'

Grant's eyes narrowed. 'Did he try — '

'For goodness sake, did nothing your sweet wife said sink in? Do not mention Liam's name again. Is that clear enough?'

'Okay, okay, I get the hint.' He held up his hands in mock surrender.

'Good. I'm going to bed. Good night,' Ellie said firmly, and left him standing there.

In her bedroom she stared at her laptop and wrestled with her conscience. She shouldn't care what Grant had discovered, but wasn't able to forget the pain in Liam's eyes when he'd mentioned his sister. She told herself she would only check her email. Twenty minutes later she'd done that, laughed at the latest viral cat videos on YouTube, and bought a pair of cute blue shoes she didn't need.

With a few clicks a large selection of pictures of Liam popped up. There were many taken from the variety of musicals he'd starred in, and they showed a very different man. He exuded a dazzling confidence with almost no hint of the pale, haunted figure she'd been drawn to yesterday. She skipped through to more recent pictures and her heart bled. Despite only knowing Liam for about thirty-six hours, Ellie trusted her instincts, and these headlines couldn't be right. How would he reply if she asked for the truth?

He'll close down and say it's none of your business.

She'd do the rest of her thinking in bed, where it was warmer. Ellie retrieved a clean pair of flannel pyjamas from the drawer and quickly got changed. Snuggled under the covers, she ran through everything again in her head. The few articles she'd skimmed through weren't the sort of things a protective brother wanted to discover about a man his sister was interested in.

Broadway star kills sister in high-speed crash.

Delaroche gets away with murder.

Cut off by his family, singing sensation goes to ground.

Marc's shrill cry pierced the still night air, and footsteps echoed through the quiet house as Tina got out of bed to see to her son. Ellie wished she could offer to help get him back to sleep, but it would bother her sister-in-law if she thought the baby had woken Ellie up. Grant was right — no one's life was perfect. It couldn't be easy for them not having a home of their own for all these months.

Ellie had left her curtains open, and the pale moonlight filling the room tempted her to get up. She crept over to the window and wished she could get dressed and go for a walk. *But you can't, because then you'd disturb everyone too.* The lack of freedom was one of the penalties for living at home, though she realised that if she'd married Will she'd be even less free. In his eyes, her underpaid teaching job couldn't possibly be rewarding, and

Ellie's intention to finish out the school year before joining him in London had irked him. He'd accused her of being afraid to live away from her family, but she'd known deep down that with the right man she wouldn't have any second thoughts.

Liam might think he was the only one with a difficult, complicated life, but he really wasn't. How she could prove it to him would keep her occupied for the rest of the night, but the one question she wouldn't ask herself was why she even cared.

9

'It there a remote chance you might offer me a cup of coffee?'

Liam ignored Maria and hung up his coat.

'I'll take that as a no.'

'Bingo.' Anything that encouraged his aunt to stay longer wasn't on his agenda. 'Let's get this over with.'

'Do you mind if I at least sit down?'

'Feel free.' Liam remained standing, determined not to let down his guard.

'Your father isn't happy with me.' Maria avoided looking at him and picked up a book on Cornish mines from the table before setting it down again. 'He blames me for the rift between y'all. I don't suppose you've spoken to Edwin?'

'Edwin? Hardly.' Cindy's husband was no fan of Liam.

'He told your father something that throws a different light on . . . what happened.' His silence made her frown. 'You aren't curious?' Maria probed. 'I'd have thought you'd be interested in anything that could clear you.'

'In case you've forgotten, the jury found me not guilty.'

'On paper. The judge made it clear that it was on a technicality because the police made mistakes when they were interviewing you. For all intents and purposes, you had 'guilty' stamped all over you.'

'How could I forget what a great support you've always been to me?'

'You were always a difficult child,' Maria answered back. 'Your sister was worth — '

'Two of me, and I should've been the one who died. I've heard it all before, thank you.' Tears burned the back of his eyes. 'Tell me what you came here to say and then get out.' He sunk into the nearest chair and cradled his head in his hands.

'Edwin admitted the other day that he and Cathy had been having problems. He says that the story you told could be true, because he'd been away on business and was due back the evening of the accident.' Maria cleared her throat. 'Your father wanted me to find out what you had to say in response.'

A surge of anger swept through Liam. 'I've already told every detail of what happened a million times. My parents, along with everyone else, preferred to believe I was lying.' He stood up and walked across the room to stand by the door. 'I've no desire to justify myself to them or anyone else this late in the game.' He put his hand on the door-knob. 'I'd like you to leave.'

'Now?' Maria protested. 'I assumed you'd let me stay the night. We could talk some more,' she pleaded.

'I'm not interested. Tell my father that if he wants to have a conversation, he can come here himself. The Red Lion pub is just around the corner on the quay and they've got rooms.'

'You've changed. You're a hard man these days.'

'I wonder why.' Liam struggled to

hide his bitterness. The worst mistake he'd ever made was in agreeing to help Cathy that fateful day. She'd had a furious row with her husband before he left on a business trip, and got it into her head to frighten Edwin by not being at home when he returned. Cathy had calmed down later and changed her mind. She'd phoned Liam because her car had broken down and she needed a lift home.

He won't ever need to know, she'd said. *I was dumb, Liam. Edwin needs me to grow up. It's time.*

Her brutal summing-up of herself and her marriage had made him unable to say no. He'd regretted it every day since.

'If that's the way you feel, I'll go.'

'It is.' Liam opened the door and a gust of cold, spitting rain stung his face.

Maria picked up her bag. 'If you change your mind, I usually have breakfast at eight. You could join me.' Out of the blue she leaned in and kissed his cheek, enveloping him in her familiar flowery scent.

'I could but I won't.'

'Good night, Liam.'

As he watched her pick her way across the cobblestones in her high heels, a wave of guilt swept through him. Then he stepped back into the house and slammed the door shut.

★　★　★

Ellie's young pupils had picked up on her cranky mood and played up the whole of Monday morning. After lunch she caved and brought out the cardboard Easter Bunnies she'd made, all ready to be decorated. She'd planned to save this activity for Thursday when the children would be bouncing off the walls before school finished for the two-week holiday, but it was more important to get through today.

Busy with supervising her five-year-olds, who were soon knee-deep in glue, glitter, and cotton balls, she didn't have time to fret about Liam. Last night she'd talked herself in and out of tackling him about his sister at least a hundred times. The only decision she did reach was that over the Easter holiday she'd find somewhere new to live, and move out.

'Miss, miss, look what Johnny did to my hair!' Mandy wailed, tugging on Ellie's skirt. The sight of the distraught little girl with cotton-wool balls stuck all over her blonde curls brought Ellie back to reality with a loud bump.

Thank heavens for washable glue. She calmed Mandy down, told the rest of the class to continue working on their rabbits, and removed Johnny to a table by himself. Ellie did the best she could, but would need to speak to Mrs. Morton after school to explain her daughter's damp, unkempt hair. Johnny's mother was another story. Mrs. Rowe was every teacher's nightmare — other children were always to blame for any trouble Johnny got himself into, never her precious son.

Somehow Ellie survived the day, but her headache ratcheted to a supersonic level as she watched the back end of the half-past-four bus disappear down the road without her. Now she'd have to wait an hour for the next one, and the wind was blowing in the perfect direction to funnel today's relentless rain straight into the bus shelter.

When she finally got off the bus in Quay Street, she abandoned the idea of putting up her umbrella because it'd be blown inside out in the gusting winds. By the time she slogged up the hill, she'd be soaked all the way through and bad-tempered. *You mean even more bad-tempered than you already are?*

A waft of tempting warmth and fragrant hot coffee drifted out of Trudgeon's café. She'd already rung her mum and told her not to wait tea on her, so another quarter of an hour wouldn't make any difference. She dived inside and dragged off her wet coat. As she hung it on the wooden rack by the door, she spotted Liam staring at her from a table over in the bay window.

'Do you want to join me before you dissolve into a puddle?'

'If you like.' Ellie refused to show too much enthusiasm after yesterday's rude dismissal. She asked Janine to bring her a latte and a fruit scone before slowly making her way across the room. 'Are you sheltering from the rain too?' Liam's hollow, lean face with its dark bruising shadows wiped away the anger she'd clung to all day. 'You look dreadful.'

A faint glimmer of amusement brightened his pallor. 'I could say a similar thing to you, but I'm too much of a gentleman.'

'I wouldn't win the Miss World contest today, that's for certain.' Her self-deprecating reply deepened his smile.

'There you go. How's little Marc doing?'

'He's absolutely adorable except for nighttimes,' she joked as Janine set down her order down. The three of them chatted for a few minutes to catch up with all the usual village gossip until Mrs. Trudgeon called out from the kitchen and told her daughter to hurry up.

'I'd better go,' Janine said. 'No rest for the wicked.'

Ellie buttered her scone and took a large bite. 'That's better. Our school lunch today was sausages and I'm not a big fan.' She cupped her hands around the chunky earthenware mug and took a cautious sip of the hot coffee. 'What've you been up to today?'

'Oh, this and that.' The darkness returned to Liam's face and he stared down at the table.

'Why did you bother to ask me to join you if you don't want to talk?' Ellie snapped. 'Trust me when I say that taking care of twenty small children on a rainy day wasn't exactly a barrel of laughs. The class demon decided it would be a good idea to glue cotton balls into a little girl's hair, which meant I had to deal with two irate mothers. I missed my bus. Got soaked. And now — '

'Now you've had to put up with an insensitive, self-absorbed man on top of everything else.' Liam leaned across the table to cover her hand with his own, and the warmth of his skin mixed with the strength pulsing through his long, shapely fingers made her forget what she'd been about to say. 'I'm sorry, Ellie.'

'Maybe neither of us is good company today,' she conceded.

'I'm guessin' that means we both need it worse than ever.' The gravelly rasp to his voice betrayed the emotions he tried so hard to cover up. 'Would you care to join me for dinner?'

'Dinner?'

'Yeah, you know, dinner. It's the meal most people eat in the evenings.' An intriguing silvery twinkle returned to his dark eyes, drawing her in against her will.

She could give a smart reply. She could be a coward and say she was too busy. Or she could answer the way she really wanted to.

10

'Please don't feel you have to be polite. I don't know what I was thinking,' Liam muttered. He knew exactly what had come over him. He'd been feeling lower than low when Ellie swept through the door, but she'd proceeded to put him in his place and drag him out of his selfish funk. Ellie somehow made everything less awful simply by being her straightforward, beautiful, kind self.

'So you're retracting the invitation? Way to make my day even worse. You're forcing me to go home and eat dried-up leftover roast beef and listen to Marc cry all evening until he finally conks out.' She scoffed, but her laughing eyes betrayed her irrepressible good humour.

'I didn't mean that,' he protested. 'I can't get anything right these days.'

'Don't be such a misery or I'll

change my mind about accepting.'

'I promise to make an effort.' Liam ached to give her some hint of truth. 'I didn't used to be this way.'

'Maybe you'll be able to tell me what changed you.'

'Maybe.'

'It's only a suggestion, not a condition.'

Gratitude flooded through him. 'You're quite a woman.'

Ellie's cheeks burned.

'I didn't mean to embarrass you.' Liam searched for the right words. 'I — '

'Shush.' She squeezed his hand. 'Let's leave. If we stay any longer, Janine will have far too much to report to my mother.' Ellie gestured over at the waitress, who was standing by the counter blatantly watching them. 'We went to school together. Trust me, what Janine doesn't know about the goings-on in Trelanow isn't worth hearing.'

'Are we considered a 'going-on'?' Liam chuckled. 'I don't think I've ever been one of those before.' His expression darkened. 'At least not in a good way, that's for sure.'

Ellie pushed back her chair and stood up. 'Come on, Mr. Gloomy.'

'Where are we going? Isn't it too early for dinner after the scone you just demolished?'

She peered out of the window. 'The rain's stopped. We'll walk out to the end of the quay and blow the cobwebs and bad tempers away.'

'Yes, ma'am.' Liam sprung to his feet. 'I'm your obedient servant.'

'For heaven's sake, don't call attention to us any more than you already have done,' she pleaded, heading towards the door and getting her coat.

'Great tea. Thanks.' Liam flashed what he'd been told was his most charming smile at Janine, surprised he still remembered how. The waitress's blush deepened as he helped Ellie on with her coat. He smoothed out the collar and allowed his hand to linger on her thick plait before letting go. 'Lead the way.'

When they stepped outside, she prodded his arm. 'What was all that in aid of?'

'I thought Janine might as well have something interesting to pass on.' Liam gave a slight shrug. 'Plus . . . ' He hesitated, afraid to step over the invisible line between them.

'Go on. Spit it out.' The slight tremble in her voice hinted at her own uncertainty.

Liam stroked his fingers down her smooth, warm cheek, lingering on her soft lips. 'I needed to touch you. You ground me.'

'Oh.'

It amused him to see her so disconcerted. *You told her the straight-forward truth. See what an amazing effect that had.* Liam tucked her hand through his arm. 'Off we go.'

Ellie somehow put one foot in front of the other until she realised they'd reached the end of the quay, though she had no memory of getting there. Something told her that Liam's artless reply to her question could be the most honest thing he'd said since they met.

'You'll freeze. Come here.' Liam stood behind her with his legs spread to steady himself against the bitter wind gusting in off the sea. Unbuttoning his coat, he wrapped himself, and it, around her. The heat from his body pressing against her seeped through Ellie and she nestled into him. 'Awesome, isn't it? Mother Nature's a pretty crazy lady.'

'She certainly is.'

They didn't speak for several minutes, and she waited for him to break the silence when he was ready.

'Do you want to tell me what Grant found out last night?'

Ellie couldn't lie.

'It's okay. Any self-respecting older brother would do the same.'

She shifted around to face him and rested her head against his shoulder. 'He didn't tell me anything, because I wouldn't listen. I told him I wouldn't be seeing you again, so it didn't matter.'

'But?'

'I admit I did a little digging around later.'

'You knew about my singing career.'

'Yes. That was the . . . easy part.' She forced herself to meet his intense gaze. 'There was a lot about your sister's death.' Ellie struggled. 'The media slammed you.'

'Yeah. Being found not guilty didn't matter.'

'Your family didn't support you.'

'That's one way of putting it.'

'I suppose it finished your stage career?' she asked.

'It finished me in every way.' Liam's cold, unemotional statement ripped at her heart. 'These last couple of days are the best I've had in two years.'

'No pressure then.' Ellie gave up a feeble attempt to smile. 'Sorry. We're supposed to be blowing away the bad stuff, not wallowing in it.'

'You'll have to make up your mind. You asked what changed me. I can either tell you the truth, or be charming and good company.' His wry smile light-ened the seriousness of the moment. 'I'm afraid you can't have it both ways. Your choice.'

Something shifted between them. Liam's offer might spoil their budding relationship, but without honesty that was meaningless. 'Go ahead.'

'Fair enough.' He glanced around. 'If it's all right with you, I suggest we go somewhere warmer. Turning into an icicle wasn't part of my plan for the day, and you're far too pretty to be one. I can fix us a hot drink in the cottage. Will that work?'

There was no going back. Once she knew his side of the story, she'd either believe him or not, and that would be it. Ellie managed to nod.

'You sure?'

'Of course.' She jutted her chin in the air. 'Unless you've changed your mind?' Her challenge brought out a ghost of Liam's smile.

'No, Ellie, I haven't.'

They strolled back along the quay as

silently as they'd walked out in the first place. As they turned into Jetty Street, Liam jolted to a stop and tightened his grip on her hand. 'Oh heck, not again,' he grumbled under his breath.

Ellie followed the path of his stare and saw an older woman outside his door. She stared across at them. 'Is that person waiting to see you?'

'Smart girl.'

'There's no need to be nasty.'

'I'm sorry.' He shoved a hand through his tousled hair. 'That's all I seem to say to you.'

'Do you know her?'

'It's my Aunt Maria.' He sighed. 'She was in London on business and came down to see me yesterday. We had a . . . disagreement, and I thought she'd left.'

'We can't just stand here, Liam. For a start we'll freeze, and the whole point of coming back was to avoid that disaster. Would you rather I went home and left you to talk your aunt in private?'

'Shoot, no.' Liam's vehemence took

her aback. 'Don't leave me to face her alone. Stay,' he pleaded.

'All right.' She slipped her hand back into his and brushed her lips in a soft kiss over his cheek. 'Come on.'

'You do like to keep me waiting, don't you?' The half-joking question was aimed at Liam, but the woman's sharp green eyes latched onto Ellie. 'I guess you were otherwise engaged.'

Liam's body stiffened against hers and she tried to be her usually friendly self in an effort to ease the tension crackling in the air around the three of them. 'It's a pleasure to meet you. I'm Ellie Teague.'

'Maria Delaroche.' She ignored Ellie's outstretched hand. 'I need to talk to my nephew.'

Liam slipped his arm around Ellie's waist and tugged her closer, his breath ragged against her face. 'You can talk to us both,' he growled.

Maria shrugged. 'Whatever. Is there any chance you might open the door before we all freeze to death?'

Ellie smiled inside and guessed Liam did the same. Maybe freezing or not would come to be their 'thing'. She guessed her curious up-and-down day was about to get even more interesting.

11

'How about I make a cup of tea?'

Liam almost managed to smile at Ellie's brave attempt to smooth things over. He was pretty much awash in the stuff after spending all afternoon in the café, but if it'd ease the worry lines etched into Ellie's forehead he'd gulp down another gallon. 'That would be great. Aunt Maria?'

'Yuck, you must be kidding. I'd rather drink dishwater,' she said with a shudder. 'Don't tell me they've anglicised you already?'

'I find I like a lot of things here more than I expected.' He stayed calm and held back on any more questions until Ellie disappeared in the direction of the kitchen. 'Why did you bother to come back?'

'I suppose you won't believe that I, along with the rest of your family, care about you?'

He snorted. 'You've got to be kidding me.'

Two bright spots of colour tinged Maria's cheeks. 'We want you to come home and talk to Edwin.'

'That's not gonna happen.'

'Don't you want to clear your name? Resume your career? Be part of the family again?'

'You don't get it, do you?' He planted himself in front of his aunt.

'Is everything all right?' Ellie asked, coming back into the room with a tray in her hands.

'No, everything isn't all right,' Liam answered.

Ellie glanced between them both and set the tray on the table. 'Do you want to tell me about it?'

'This is a private conversation,' Maria protested.

'Yeah, I do, Ellie.' Liam had put his aunt on the spot to see what happened. 'Go ahead, explain why I'm a pariah.'

'Me?'

'Yeah, you.' He flopped down on the

sofa. 'Thanks for the tea, Ellie.' He picked up a mug. 'Don't be shy, Aunt Maria.'

'How much does she know?'

'Her *name* is Ellie, and feel free to ask her yourself. She doesn't bite.'

Ellie turned stern. 'That's enough from both of you. I wasn't invited here to be insulted.' She focused on Liam's aunt. 'We both . . . care about Liam and want the best for him. Surely we're on the same side?'

'I'm sorry,' Liam mumbled. 'I never meant to drag you into this mess.'

'Sure looks as though coming here might've been good for you.' Maria gave him a searching look. 'I like her. She's got backbone.'

You really shouldn't have said that.

'Excuse me, but I'd prefer it if you didn't discuss me as though I'm not here,' Ellie bristled. 'Why don't you sit down, Maria, and start at the beginning. I only did a very quick check online last night, and we all know how the press exaggerates.' She perched on the sofa next to Liam and reached over to hold his hand.

'If you insist.' Maria chose one of the wing-backed chairs. 'It's pretty straight-forward. Liam picked up his sister, Cathy, in Baton Rouge where she'd been . . . staying. On their way back to New Orleans they had a wreck and she died.' Tears trickled down Maria's cheeks. 'He ignored the appalling weather forecast and raced the car on the icy roads. When the case came to court, the jury was instructed to find Liam not guilty because the police had questioned him under debatable cir-cumstances.'

'Debatable?'

'I'd call laid up in a hospital bed with a broken leg, broken wrist, multiple lacerations to the face and back, plus doped up to the eyeballs with pain-killers debatable.' His gravelly voice tore at Ellie and she struggled to keep her focus.

'That doesn't alter the facts though, does it?' Maria's anger erupted.

'No,' Liam said. 'Cathy's still dead.'

'But I don't understand,' Ellie interrupted. 'Why were you driving if the weather was so bad?'

Liam pulled away from her. 'There's no excuse, all right?' He fixed his searing dark glare on his aunt. 'It makes no difference what Edwin's saying now. The reason we were on the road is irrelevant. I should have refused Cathy but I didn't. End of story.' His expression hardened as he turned back to Ellie. 'You don't need to get mixed up with me. Go on home. You're a great woman. Go find yourself a decent guy.' He stood up. 'Aunt Maria, I appreciate you making the effort, but you can tell everyone I don't need to be babied.' He cleared his throat. 'I'll get on with my life and they can get on with theirs.'

Ellie couldn't decide whether she wanted to shake Liam or hug him. The one thing he plainly wasn't doing was getting on with his life. 'That's it?' She fought to hold her voice steady. 'You're sending both of us away so you can keep feeling sorry for yourself?' Liam recoiled but she forced herself not to back down. Every good teacher knew when to push a pupil and when to draw back. 'I'm going, if that's what you want.' Quietly she gathered her coat and handbag. 'If you change your mind, you know where I am.' He fixed his gaze on the carpet, and she gained a measure of satisfaction from the fact he couldn't look at her. 'Maria, thank you for trying to help. Have a safe journey home.'

'I'll try. I'm staying at the Red Lion again tonight and I'll head back to London in the morning.'

Ellie nodded and left, latching the door quietly behind her. Halfway along the quay she remembered they'd never got around to having dinner. The idea of eating turned her stomach, but so did the thought of facing her family. Going to the Red Lion wasn't an option because of the chance of running into Maria again, which left the Green Dragon — not her favourite place, but it would do for her purpose.

As soon as she stepped inside, a wave of welcoming heat enveloped her.

'Well, look who it isn't.' Will sat at the bar smiling right at her. 'Join me.'

Agreeing was easier than getting into a public argument, so Ellie made her way over.

'White wine?'

'I suppose.'

'Where's your Yank tonight?'

'Where's Lavinia?' she tossed back at him.

'Gone back to London.' He took a long draw of his pint and she couldn't help smiling. Will would never drink beer in front of his fancy London friends. 'I've got the week off for Easter and haven't seen much of my parents recently, so I thought I'd stay.'

The barman set a glass down in front of Ellie and Will paid before she could get her purse out. 'I've answered *your* question.'

Ellie sipped her wine. 'Liam's a friend. That's all.'

'Really?'

'Yes, really.'

'It didn't look that way on Saturday when he displayed his kissing skills in front of everyone in the Red Lion.'

She was determined not to get into a slanging match with Will. She'd been the cause of enough gossip recently. 'I'm not in the market for anything serious, and neither is he.' She gulped down the rest of her wine and slid off the stool. 'Thanks for the drink.'

'You're going already?'

'Yes, it's time I was heading home.'

'I'll walk you up the hill.' Before she could protest, he stood up and slipped his coat back on. Ellie's cheeks heated. The dark brown leather jacket had been her Christmas gift to him a couple of years ago.

'You don't have to.'

'I'm perfectly aware of that.' Will smiled. 'I want to.'

Without speaking, she headed for the door, leaving him to follow along behind. They fell into step and wandered along by the harbour wall, something they'd done a thousand times before. Ellie smelled his familiar clean, spicy cologne in the crisp night air, and tears stung her eyes as years of overwhelming memories flooded back.

'I never meant to put you down, Ellie.' Will picked up her hand and stroked her cold fingers.

'You made me feel stupid and unsophisticated.'

He shook his head. 'I was an idiot.'

'Yes, you were,' Ellie agreed, and was surprised by his burst of laughter. Laughing at himself was never Will's strong point.

'I don't suppose . . . ' he began.

'What?'

'You'd consider, um, being . . . friends again.' Will rested a finger on her chin, tilting her face to meet his questioning gaze. 'And maybe more again one day?'

Her lingering anger at Liam . . . the soft moonlight . . . the long history they shared. Ellie's head swam in a confused mess.

'Please say yes, Ellie.'

She sucked in a deep breath and prepared to make perhaps the second biggest mistake of her life.

12

Liam yanked his coat collar up around his neck to keep out the biting wind and shoved his hands deep in his pockets. He deserved to stand here in the shadows cast by the old buildings and shiver while he watched Ellie. The moonlight mocked him by catching the glint of her thick gold hair, highlighting the curve of her beautiful smile and showing Will Burton staring adoringly at her.

Liam couldn't watch them any longer. He turned away and trudged back to the cottage. He considered the bottle of whisky he'd bought yesterday, but left it unopened and instead spread out his drawing paper and charcoal pencils on the kitchen table. He drew Ellie, and only Ellie, because she filled his mind. At some point he made a pot of coffee, because tea didn't work for a serious caffeine fix, and it kept him awake until he couldn't keep his eyes open any longer.

A loud banging noise shook him awake and for a second he couldn't work out where he was. Someone shouted his name and Liam dragged himself to his feet. He stumbled out to the front door and fumbled with the lock.

'It's Matt.'

'All right, hang on.' He flung back the door and registered Matt's worried expression. 'What's up?'

'It's Ms. Delaroche. We thought you ought to know she's been taken to the hospital.'

'Come in.'

'Better not. I'm fair soaked.' Rain ran out of his dark hair and he dripped all over the mat.

'Don't be an idiot.' Liam pulled the barman in over the step. 'Get rid of your coat.' He ran to the kitchen for a towel. 'Here, dry yourself off.'

Matt cracked a smile. 'Cheers, Dad.'

'Sit down and tell me what's goin' on.' Liam dropped down into the nearest chair and listened with a growing sense of panic.

'We were locking up the pub for the night and heard a loud thump upstairs. I ran up and found her lying on the floor outside the bathroom,' Matt explained. 'She were a bit shaken up, and we called the ambulance because she wasn't making sense when I talked to her and seemed confused.' He rubbed the towel over his wet hair. 'The paramedics reckoned it was some sort of stroke.'

Liam cursed under his breath. It didn't matter what anyone else said, deep down he knew that worrying about him had brought this on. 'Where've they taken her?'

'Treliske Hospital. It's down near Truro.' Matt patted his arm. 'They'll take good care of your aunt.'

'I must go.' Liam checked his watch. 'Is there anywhere here I can get a taxi this late?'

'I'll run you down there.'

'I can't — '

'Don't be daft,' Matt declared. 'By the time you get someone from St. Austell to pick you up we can be there. There's no traffic this time of night.' He stood up. 'Get your coat. My car's down around the back of the pub.'

Liam's attempt to thank him was brushed off, so he grabbed his coat and wallet and the keys to lock up the cottage. He dismissed the thought of ringing Ellie before it could take root. 'Let's go.'

⋆ ⋆ ⋆

Ellie tossed uselessly in the bed all night, and just before six o'clock finally gave up hope of getting any sleep and crawled out. Before the break-up with Will she'd routinely run a couple of miles before going to work, but she'd slackened off and could feel the difference. After tracking down her long-abandoned trainers in the back of the wardrobe, she finished getting dressed and crept downstairs.

The street lights cast a muted yellow glow over the deserted road, and Ellie stopped outside the gate to stretch and warm up. She breathed in the cool morning air, fresh and crisp from the overnight rain, and without wasting another minute set off down the hill. Running along by the harbour, she spotted the butcher unloading a de-livery lorry and Mrs. Hawkins in the corner shop sorting out the news-papers.

Jetty Street wasn't on her usual route, but she turned at the corner and stopped on the pavement outside Mrs. Pearce's cottage. Liam's lights were on and she peeked in through his open curtains. Then she froze as he glanced up from the sofa and stared right at her. She couldn't walk away.

Liam ignored her first knock but she persisted. 'Yeah?' he growled as he flung back the door. He still wore yesterday's black ill-fitting clothes, and the swath of dark stubble shadowing his jaw did nothing to enhance his grim appearance.

'Are you all right?'

'Who, me? I'm a barrel of laughs.' Liam's humourless smile cut through her. 'Next question?'

'I'm sorry I didn't mean to . . . disturb you.'

'You're a bit late for that, sweetheart.'

'I'll leave you alone.' Ellie stumbled over her words. 'I need to get ready for school.'

'Good idea,' Liam replied. But before he could close the door, she stuck out her hand to stop him.

'Is something wrong?' she asked.

'Wrong? Why would anything be wrong?' Liam's cynical laughter turned her stomach. 'Let's see. My aunt is in the hospital after having a stroke. I'll have to call my father later to tell him I might've killed another member of our family. Plus the woman who . . . befriended me took my stupid words to heart and cleared off back to her old boyfriend. Life's just peachy.'

'Are you talking about Maria?' She settled on the least contentious subject.

'Yeah, late last night.'

'Do you want to tell me about it?' She dared to touch his arm and got a small measure of comfort from the fact that he didn't pull away. 'I could come in and make us some tea.'

'The British cure-all.' One corner of his mouth twitched with a flicker of amusement.

'It certainly is.'

'Fine.' His resigned sigh wasn't an enthusiastic invitation, but she'd take what she could get. 'You know where the kitchen is.'

Ellie breezed in past him. 'Have you eaten?'

'No.'

She plastered on a cheerful smile. 'Is it a forlorn hope to think you've got any food in the house?'

'Yes.'

'Yes you do, or yes it's a forlorn hope?'

'The latter.' A faint gleam brightened his hollow eyes.

'In that case, we'll drink and starve.'

'I could go to the shop and pick up something if they're open this early.'

'Thanks for offering, but I don't have time. I've got to catch the eight o'clock bus into work.' Ellie made a beeline for the kitchen and Liam followed along behind. She tried to work around him, too acutely aware of his physical presence to concentrate. 'Ouch,' she yelped, splashing boiling water on her right hand.

'Are you all right?' He moved the kettle out of her reach and led her over to the sink. Then he turned on the tap and let the cold water run over her tender skin. His breath warmed her neck, and unconsciously she leaned back close enough to feel the rapid thud of his heartbeat against her spine. 'Why did you go back to him?' he whispered. 'Make me understand.'

Ellie turned to face Liam. 'Were you spying on me last night?'

'No, I . . . ' Liam's lean, warm fingers lingered on her cheek. 'I needed to talk to you and apologise, but I saw you with Will on the quay and guessed there wasn't much point.'

Could she lay herself bare and admit the complete truth?

13

'I shouldn't have asked. You don't have to explain yourself to me.' Liam struggled to sound reasonable while dying a little more inside with each additional second that Ellie remained silent. 'It's none of my business. You asked about Maria.'

'I do want to hear about your aunt, but . . . I need to make something clear first.'

Liam recognised a dismissal when he heard one.

'Don't jump to conclusions like you obviously did last night.' She wagged her finger at him.

'What was I supposed to think?'

'You weren't *supposed* to think anything.' A faint smile brightened her eyes. 'I didn't know I was being watched.'

Ellie's characteristic rose scent enveloped him and Liam hooked his thumbs in his pockets to keep from touching her. He listened to her halting explanation about leaving him and going to the Green Dragon.

'Will seemed like the man he used to be.' Her eyes glazed with tears and she blinked them away. 'He apologised for being unkind to me, and . . . ' Ellie's voice cracked.

'Asked for a second chance?' That wasn't hard to guess, because it was why Liam had run after her in the first place.

'I came this close to saying yes.' She pinched together two fingers. 'We'd shared so much that was good. But in the end I couldn't.'

Liam was afraid to ask if her decision had anything to do with him.

'It'd be going backwards, and I refuse to do that any longer. In the long run, nothing would be any different.' Her wry smile encouraged him. 'Will told me what he thought I wanted to hear, but I know him too well. I discovered that his new girlfriend dumped him. Will's cosmopolitan shine obviously wore off in the Red Lion.'

Liam bit back a smile.

'Don't smirk.'

'I wasn't.'

She prodded his chest. 'Inside here you did.'

'Maybe.'

'So why *did* you come after me?' Ellie persisted.

Because I'd been dumb and wanted to throw myself at your feet. I need help and I need you. The words stuck in his throat.

'You disappoint me. I didn't have you marked down as a coward.' She stepped away from him and bumped up against the sink. 'I'm glad I was honest with you. It makes me feel much better.'

'It isn't easy,' he complained.

'Really? You could've fooled me. I thought it was an absolute breeze to bare my soul to a man I barely know.'

Liam threw up his hands. 'Okay, okay, I give in.' A flash of triumph lit up her eyes. 'God, you're tough. Nobody would think you dealt with little kids every day.'

'There speaks someone who's obviously not a teacher or a parent.'

'How about that cup of tea?' he suggested.

'Tea?'

'Yeah, you know, the hot wet stuff you were going to fix when we started to talk about . . . other things.' He pointed to the kitchen table. 'We can sit and talk while we drink.' Ellie gave him a suspicious stare. 'I'm not putting it off.' He drew a finger across his throat. 'Promise.'

'Did you know the saying 'cross my heart and hope to die' originated in the very early years of the twentieth century in the form of a religious oath using the sign of the cross to swear someone was telling the truth?'

Liam's bemusement must've showed, because a soft pink blush crept up her neck and coloured her cheeks. 'I know. I can't help it.' Ellie laughed. 'I'll make the tea. You can sit down and start talking.'

'Yes, ma'am.' He ducked to avoid her half-hearted swipe at his arm, then followed her orders and stretched out his aching legs. 'I was an idiot yesterday and came searching for you for forgiveness. I need help and I need you.' He blurted everything out before his overtired brain could attempt to edit the simple truth.

The wet teabag dropped out of Ellie's hand and splattered on the floor. 'Oh.'

'I can't forget what you said — that I was sending you and Maria away so I could carry on feeling sorry for myself. You nailed it.'

'I didn't mean — '

'Don't you dare take it back. You were right.' Liam's intense stare kept her silent. 'I've completely wasted the last two years of my life, and that's as big a crime as anything I committed in the first place.' He sucked in a deep audible breath. 'I'm begging for your help.'

Ellie leaned across the table and laid her warm hands on top of his. 'There's no begging necessary. All you had to do was ask.'

'Really?'

'Really.' She wished she didn't have to rush off. 'I can't afford to miss my bus, but I haven't heard about your aunt yet.'

'She was doing well when I phoned this morning. The doctor said they'd be doing more tests, but all the initial indications point to what they call a TIA, a transient ischemic attack. I think it's sort of a warning rather than a real stroke, but I'll find out more when I see her later.'

'Oh right. My father had one of those last year. At first they thought he'd had a stroke too, but the symptoms disappeared very quickly and the tests confirmed it was a TIA.' Ellie reluctantly stood up. 'Would you like me to come back here tonight and cook dinner for us?'

'You mean you can do more than boil water?' Liam teased.

'Cheeky devil.'

'I've never been anyone's 'cheeky devil' before.' His cheeks heated.

'There's a first time for everything.'

Liam came to stand in front of her, and his lazy smile warmed her all the way to her toes. He slid his hands around her waist and tugged her close enough to kiss. 'You have no idea how many firsts I've already celebrated with you,' he murmured. 'Go and make more Easter Bunnies.'

Ellie shuddered. 'Thanks, but I had quite enough of that yesterday.'

At the front door neither wanted to be the first to say goodbye.

'Get some sleep and make sure you eat properly before you go back to Truro.' Ellie held up her hand. 'And don't 'yes, ma'am' me either.'

'No, ma'am,' Liam chuckled, the laughter lightening his thin, drawn features and taking years off him. 'I promise I'll be a good boy.' He sneaked another kiss and she didn't have the heart to push him away. 'Very good.'

Ellie hesitated, unsure whether to say

what was on her mind.

'Spit it out.'

It bemused her how this man who'd only known her a grand total of four days could pick up on her thoughts so fast. She'd known Will for nearly twenty-five years and he still didn't understand her that well. Last night had proved it.

'When you speak to your father, please don't take all the blame on yourself for Maria's illness. You've burdened yourself with enough . . . rightly or wrongly. Simply give him the facts.'

Liam frowned. 'I'm not sure he'll agree with you, but we'll see.' He opened the door and peered outside. 'No rain. Isn't that against the law for Cornwall?'

'It's March. What did you expect? Wait until the summer. It's amazingly beautiful then, and . . . ' Ellie pressed her lips shut. Implying that Liam would still be in Trelanow when summer rolled around was wishful thinking on her part.

He instantly wrapped his strong warm arms around her and she almost forgot to breathe. 'Don't apologise. My plans aren't set in stone. Can we leave it there for a while?'

'Of course,' she whispered.

'You'd better leave while I've still got the willpower to let you go.' He eased away. 'We'll compare notes on our days later. I'd be willing to bet you'll win on the 'having fun' stakes.'

'Maybe.'

The first tinkling notes of the title song from *Oklahoma* interrupted them and Liam pulled out his phone, grimacing at the display.

'Your father?'

'Got it in one.'

'You ought to answer him. I must go.' Before she could be tempted to linger, Ellie popped a quick kiss on his cheek and hurried away. She'd have to wait until tonight to satisfy her curiosity.

14

'Do you know where your Aunt Maria's gone to? She should be back in London by now, but I can't track her down, and her phone keeps going to voicemail,' Liam's father thundered down the line.

'Hi, Dad. I was going to call you later.'

'Why?'

He didn't bother to say 'because we're family and family keep in touch'. They'd sadly abandoned that pretence after Cathy died. Liam took a couple of deep steadying breaths. 'Maria's not very well. She's — '

'You've upset her, haven't you? If anything happens to her, I'll never — '

' — forgive me,' Liam finished his father's sentence. Ellie was living in cloud cuckoo land if she thought Edouard wouldn't blame him for this. 'Yeah, I know. Are you gonna listen, or carry on berating me before you even know what happened?'

A moment's silence hung between them.

'Back off, son. I'm worried. That's all.' His voice cracked.

Liam's eyes filled with tears as he heard his father's unspoken words: *You'd be the same if it was your sister.* 'Aunt Maria is in the local hospital here but she's gonna be okay.' He crossed his fingers. Before Edouard could bombard him with questions, he quietly explained everything he knew.

'I'm not surprised. Maria's doctor warned her only the other day she was a heart attack or stroke waiting to happen, but she wouldn't listen to him or me.'

Runs in the family.

'I'll check on flights and be there tomorrow if I can.'

'Why don't you wait until I've visited her at the hospital this afternoon? I'll talk to the doctors and see what they have to say.'

'I guess I could.'

His father's agreement shocked Liam. He hadn't thought for one second that Edouard would trust him to take care of his aunt's welfare even for a few hours.

'Had you . . . um, talked any before she was taken ill?'

'Yeah.'

'And?'

Liam could make this hard or get it over with. He was too tired to drag it out any longer. 'We spoke, and she passed on Edwin's message . . . and yours. We disagreed. The stress from all that could've had a negative effect on her, and if it did I'm sorry.'

'It's more likely because of the extra weight she was carrying around, the fried foods she insisted on eating, and the careless way she forgot to take her blood pressure medication most of the time.' The surprising response floored Liam. 'I'm not saying the other trouble helped any, but don't beat yourself up over this.' Liam's silence earned a faint chuckle from his father. 'Thought I was going to launch into you, I suppose?'

'It'd be par for the course.' Another heavy silence dragged on, and Liam wondered who'd break it first.

'We've got to talk, son.' Edouard sighed. 'Not today. But soon.'

'Yeah,' Liam growled, not willing to sound too enthusiastic but not stupid enough to close the door on the possibility of some level of reconciliation either.

'I'd better get on up to bed or your mother will fret.'

'I'm going to try to sleep some too. I only got a few naps at the hospital last night.'

'Take care of yourself, Liam.' His father's gruff order touched him. 'Call me later.' Edouard hung up, and for a few seconds Liam didn't move. That hadn't gone at all how he'd expected.

Tired or hungry? He struggled to decide which was the priority and settled on sleep, because his eyes were fighting a losing battle to stay open. He made his way upstairs and flopped on top of his bed without bothering to undress. In the last few seconds before giving in to exhaustion, he remembered to set the alarm on his watch so he wouldn't oversleep and miss visiting time. That wouldn't go down well.

★ ★ ★

Ellie struggled to hide her surprise when Liam opened the door. The freshly washed hair, clean shave and non-black clothes all combined to push away the general air of weariness she associated with him. *Who's the vampire?* Patsy wouldn't say that tonight. A rush of blood heated Ellie's face and neck as an amused smile lit up Liam's face.

'I was afraid they'd mistake me for a patient and keep me at the hospital if I didn't tidy up before visiting my aunt.'

His self-deprecating comment made Ellie laugh. 'You obviously got away with it.'

'Sure did.' Liam's smile deepened. 'I didn't want to miss the gourmet feast.'

'Feast?' Ellie frowned, and then it clicked he was referring to the dinner she'd offered to cook. 'Oh, dear, I'd better lower your expectations right away. Just because I said I could do better than boiling water doesn't mean I'm any competition for Nigella.'

'Whoever she is.'

'A celebrity cook who's almost as well known for being glamorous as she is for her food.' Her cheeks burned. Ellie hoped he didn't think she wasn't begging for a compliment. When she got home from school it had come down to either buying the ingredients for dinner or changing, and the food had won out. This meant her hair was still tied back in its sensible plait and she wore the grey trousers and plain navy jumper she'd worked in all day.

'You rushed here to be with me. Nigella didn't.' Liam lowered his mouth to hers and pressed a soft kiss on her lips. 'If it wouldn't embarrass, you I'd tell you how beautiful you are.'

She stumbled over her attempt to

reply, bewitched by his sparkling silver-grey eyes focused steadily on her. What did a girl say to a man who disguised a compliment in the form of a denial? 'I'd better get on with dinner. You can tell me how Maria is while I cook,' she gabbled.

'Dinner. Good idea,' he said, but made no move to let go of her. 'You must've been good karma this morning.'

'Why?'

'My father was . . . reasonable when we spoke.'

Ellie beamed. 'That's wonderful.'

'He's not exactly hanging out the flags and welcoming home the prodigal son any time soon, but at least we managed to have a conversation without yelling at each other.' Liam's wry smile revealed his pleasure. 'Let's go back to the kitchen.'

'You smooth talker. Do you charm all the women that way?'

A shadow crossed his face. 'It's been years since I charmed anybody. I wouldn't know where to start.'

He was totally wrong, but today wasn't the time to tell him that. Ellie snatched a quick kiss and pulled away. 'Can you chop onions?' Liam frowned. 'You know, the bulbous root vegetables that make you cry?'

'I'm never sure where the conversation is going next with you.'

'Keeps you on your toes.' She laughed. 'It comes from being around five-year-olds all day. Most of them have the attention span of a frenetic gnat.'

Liam held up his large, slender hands. 'These can reduce an onion to a pile of perfect dice in the blink of an eye.'

'Another of your talents?'

He winked. 'Come with me and find out.'

★   ★   ★

Liam leaned against the kitchen counter and took a sip of wine. 'This isn't bad. There wasn't much choice at the local shop.' He'd prepped all the vegetables for Ellie and was now enjoying watching her cook.

'Tell me about Maria,' she invited, starting to stir fry the chicken she'd diced and marinated in a spicy peanut sauce.

'She's doing well and is anxious to get out of hospital, but her blood pressure is still too high. After a load of tests they say it definitely was a TIA. Your father seems to be doing okay now after his?'

She nodded. 'He's had to make some lifestyle changes though. He altered his diet and goes for a walk every day. Takes paracetamol too every morning. They warned him if he didn't change things, then next time it would likely be a proper heart attack or stroke.'

'Yeah.' Liam pinched a couple of carrot strips from the chopping board and popped them into his mouth. 'Dad told me my aunt's had high blood pressure for years, doesn't take her meds, eats all the wrong stuff, and the last time she exercised Reagan was president.'

'That's — '

'Stupid, I know.' He smiled. 'A lot of us get advice but we don't always take it.'

An easy quiet fell between them as Ellie methodically carried on cooking. 'Lay the table. It's almost ready.' She caught his eye and they both burst out laughing. Both of them knew he'd been about to say 'yes, ma'am' and she would've teased him again.

'This is a heck of a lot better than boiling water,' Liam commented a few minutes later, scooping up another delicious forkful. 'You're a dark horse. What else don't I know about you?'

'Probably as much as I don't know about you.'

'Touché.' Liam raised his wineglass in a mock toast. 'Maybe we could swap notes.' He cracked a sly smile. 'Although not music ones in your case.'

Ellie playfully smacked his arm. 'For that remark you get to wash the dishes.'

'It's my specialty.' He'd play along with her obvious desire to keep things light-hearted between them for now. 'Did I tell you Harry Richards has been in touch? My presence is required at choir practice tomorrow evening.' The change of topic worked and Ellie relaxed again. *Remember, Liam, the woman's not for rushing.*

15

'Tomorrow? Oh, right.' Liam frowned at the doctor. 'Are you sure that's not too soon? It's an arduous journey back to the States.'

'I don't recommend that Ms. Delaroche returns home for at least a week. She needs to rest, plus I want to see her again before we clear her for travelling,' he explained. 'I assumed she'd stay with you.'

'With me?'

'I understand she has no other contacts here, and a hotel really wouldn't be suitable.' Liam caught the hint of censure in the doctor's voice. 'We would've released her today, but I want her blood pressure to be more stable, so I think tomorrow is realistic.'

'Of course.' His aunt wouldn't be happy about the situation, but there was no other option.

'If you ring about noon tomorrow, I'll have finished with my rounds, and the ward staff will know if I've scheduled Ms. Delaroche to be released. If you have a word with the nurse now, she'll give you the diet sheet so you can get some things in ready. We'll give you more information on her follow-up care when you collect her.'

Liam groaned inwardly. If he was stuck with trying to persuade his aunt to obey the doctor's orders, it could start off World War Three. 'Thanks. I'll go and break her the good news.' The doctor's eyebrows rose and Liam guessed he hadn't managed to hide his doubts.

Entering the ward, he waved across the long room at his aunt, and Maria glowered back at him. As soon as he reached the foot of her bed, she started on him.

'One of the nurses told me there's a shop downstairs. For heaven's sake, get down there and buy me some sand-wiches and a supply of chocolate before

I starve to death,' she ordered, sounding so much like his father. 'You should've seen the pathetic lunch they gave me. Grilled chicken. Salad with no dressing. And steamed broccoli. Steamed broccoli! It wasn't enough to keep a fly alive.'

It plainly did the trick though, because you're still kicking and screaming.

'When I tell your father how I'm being treated, he'll fly over here and sort them out,' she snorted.

'I'm sure he'll completely support the hospital's efforts to prevent you from having a serious stroke or heart attack another time.' His aunt's face turned purple, and Liam was afraid he'd gone too far. As calmly as he could, he repeated the doctor's words and waited for them to sink in.

'A week? With you?'

'It's that or a nursing home. Take your pick.'

Maria slumped back on the pillows. 'Fine. I guess it'll have to be your place.'

Liam hadn't expected gratitude and plainly wouldn't get it. 'I'll be back tomorrow and hopefully spring you out of here.' He tried to jolly her along but she wasn't having any of it, and turned her face away to the window.

He checked his watch as he hurried out into the corridor. If he was lucky, he could be back in Trelanow in time to give his father an update before meeting Ellie's bus. They hadn't made any plans, but he really wanted to see her again. Tonight's choir practice was due to start at seven o'clock, and although he had no desire to sing in public again, Liam couldn't break his hastily made promise to Harry. He'd put his limited amount of charm to work and hopefully persuade Ellie to eat an early dinner with him. After two years of virtual hibernation, he'd come to the belated conclusion it was time to live again. He didn't know yet what shape or form it might take, but trying was a start.

★ ★ ★

'Oh, I didn't expect to see you again.' Ellie stepped out of the way to let the other passengers off the bus.

'Why not? You didn't think I'd take no for an answer that easily, did you?' Will's open smile was at odds with his sharp-eyed gaze. 'Come on, Ellie — '

'You got to know when to quit, pal.' Liam appeared out of nowhere and draped his arm around Ellie's shoulder, giving a quick hard squeeze. 'You ready, honey?'

She opened her mouth to ask what on earth he was talking about and was kissed instead. Not a simple friendly kiss, but one that lasted long enough to make his point. A flash of anger shifted across Will's face before he wiped it away.

'Excuse us, but we've got places to go.' Liam steered Ellie across the street and hesitated outside the Red Lion. 'How about an early dinner?'

'Why?'

'Um, early because I've got choir practice at seven thanks to Harry.

142

Dinner because it's — '

' — the meal most people eat in the evenings.' She smiled as she finished his sentence. 'I need to call my mum first.'

'Sure. Say hello to the lovely Jennifer from me.'

Ellie rolled her eyes as she pulled her phone from her bag. After a quick conversation, she tossed Liam a stern glare. 'Before we go in to eat, you can explain your behaviour back there.'

'You didn't want to be bothered by Will again, did you?'

'No.' Her colour rose. 'But I am a grown woman and perfectly capable of telling a man to clear off all by myself.' Liam tried to speak but she ploughed on. 'I've proved that. Ask anyone around the village.'

'I sure am sorry. I didn't mean — '

'Oh, forget it,' Ellie brushed him off. 'You can attempt to get back into my good graces by treating me to gammon steak with all the trimmings.'

'I'm not even goin' to ask what trimmings are. I guess it's another

143

British thing.' The teasing sparkle in his eyes intensified. 'After you.' He swung open the door and stood back to let her go first. Liam rested a gentle hand at the base of her spine, protective but unobtrusive. 'How about I get our drinks and order while you track us down a table?'

'Thanks. I'll have a glass of chardonnay, and tell Matt I'd like one egg and one pineapple with the gammon.' She said it on purpose to confuse him. 'He'll know what you mean.'

Liam muttered something under his breath, and she'd take a guess that it was something along the lines of being glad *someone* understood her.

It was still early, so Ellie was able to get her favourite table close to the fire. Late March in Cornwall was always unpredictable, and this Easter was doomed to be rainy and cold. It would put a damper on the number of visitors who often decided on last-minute holidays depending on the weather forecast.

'Matt said our food will be about ten

minutes.' Liam set down their drinks and sat next to Ellie on the bench. She didn't object when he slipped his arm around her shoulders, and she nestled into his solid warmth without caring who saw them. 'You always smell so good. The perfect combination of roses and beautiful woman.'

She wasn't sure how to react. Ellie had never been good at accepting compliments, probably because she didn't receive that many.

'I'm only telling it as I see it, honey. I'm not a flirt. Never have known how.'

'Me neither,' she whispered.

'One gammon and one vegetable soup.' Matt set the dishes down in front of them. 'How're you two doing tonight?' The unsubtle inference behind his words made Ellie's cheeks flame.

'Fine, mate, thanks,' Liam answered, seemingly unperturbed.

'I hear the word's got around that you're joining the choir,' Matt teased. 'I expect a large number of local women will get a burning desire to sing on

Easter Sunday.' He gave Ellie's arm a playful jab. 'You aren't one of them, are you?'

'Hardly,' she scoffed.

'Good. Two of the stained-glass windows are already broken and need to be replaced. We don't want any more to get damaged, do we, Liam?'

Ellie had known Matt all her life and had no qualms about telling him in no uncertain terms to clear off and leave them alone.

'I thought he'd never stop plaguing us.'

'One of the penalties of village life,' Ellie commented with a shrug. She peered at his frugal meal, a bowl of soup and a wheat roll. 'Is that all you're having?'

'I never eat much before I sing.'

'This isn't Broadway, you know.'

'Yeah, but it's what I do.' Lines furrowed his forehead. 'Don't you put as much effort into teaching baby Marc as when you've got a class of twenty to handle?'

'Yes, but — '

'There's your answer then.' He pointed to her plate. 'Those are trimmings?'

Ellie grinned. 'Gammon steak is always served with chips, mushrooms, peas, grilled tomato, pineapple and a fried egg. It's an unwritten rule.'

'That figures.'

'But some people like two pineapple slices and no egg or the other way around.'

'Naturally.' He struggled to keep a straight face.

'Stop mocking. That's quite enough about our strange English habits. How's your aunt doing today? Will they send her home soon?'

Liam set down his spoon. 'Yeah. That's the problem.'

'Can I do anything to help?'

'You may wish you hadn't asked,' he warned.

'Go ahead. It can't be any worse than dealing with Marc when he's got an attack of colic.'

Liam lifted his eyes skyward. 'I wouldn't be so sure.'

Maria hadn't exactly been overly friendly towards Ellie, who wondered what she might be about to let herself in for.

16

Liam wasn't sure how he got out of the choir practice alive, but he finally made his escape and reached the cottage door with extreme relief. He'd received at least six requests for private singing lessons — a couple of them might be genuine, but Liam suspected the rest were contrived to corner him on his own. Harry owed him big time for this.

Ellie stopped in the middle of dusting the table. 'There you are. How did it go?'

Guilt slammed through Liam. He shouldn't be taking advantage of her this way. 'I'm sorry for landing you — '

'Stop right there,' she ordered. 'You didn't force me. I offered.' Ellie gave a sly smile. 'Of course, you did bribe me with gammon steak and — '

'All the trimmings.' Liam laughed. He couldn't seem to help it around her.

'Do you want a cup of tea? I know I could murder one.'

'You sit down and I'll fix it,' he said firmly. 'I'll tell you all about my experiences with the choir mafia.'

'Oh dear, was it that bad?'

Liam remembered that Ellie knew all these people, so he needed to be careful what he said. The last thing he wanted was to upset her.

'Don't be silly. Nothing you say will go outside these walls. There's no harm in a little gossip.'

'Isn't there?'

She stepped in front of him and he couldn't avoid her piercing blue eyes. 'I know you've been through the wringer, but you've got to stop taking everything so seriously. A little fun never hurt anyone. Whatever goes on here is between us, and that's private, right?'

He suspected he was being asked a whole lot more than simply whether he'd keep their innocent chatter to himself. 'Yeah. What we have is between us and . . . it's good.'

'It certainly is.' Her mouth curved into a smile, and Liam couldn't resist pressing a gentle kiss onto her soft lips. He wrapped his arms around her, and as she rested her head on his shoulder it took him a few seconds to pinpoint the feeling surging through him. It was happiness. He'd come perilously close to forgetting how that felt.

'Tea?'

'In a minute,' he whispered, hating to break the moment while knowing he should for both their sakes. He breathed in her heady scent and then forced himself to drop his hands back down. 'You shall have tea.' He rifled in his voluminous coat pocket for a small foil-wrapped package before tossing the coat on the back of the sofa. 'With homemade cherry and walnut cake courtesy of . . . Marlene Hicks. At least, I think that's what she said her name was.'

'Yummy. She's a good cook and always wins prizes in the garden show when it's our Feast Week.' Ellie smothered a giggle. 'Of course, she's also closer to fifty than forty and has never been married, but hasn't given up hope.'

'I hardly know what to ask first.' Liam shook his head. 'We'll leave aside Marlene's interest in changing her marital status. Tell me what a Feast Week is and why someone would enter a cake in a garden show.' He grinned. 'Flour and flowers might sound the same, but unless England is different from the rest of the world, they're total opposites.'

'I think we're at cross purposes again. I'm going to stick the kettle on.' Ellie giggled. 'No, I'm not about to glue the kettle to the wall or anywhere else, merely turn it on to boil.'

Liam threw his hands in the air. 'I wasn't going to say a word. I'm confused enough already. Tea and cake it is.' He followed her into the kitchen and lounged against the countertop while she got busy. Patiently she explained about the week-long celebration every

August centred on when the village church was started.

'I suppose that was back in the Dark Ages?' Liam joked.

'Not quite. I think it's seven hundred and fifty-three years, something like that.'

Ellie's casual assumption of her long heritage made him envious. He'd moved around so much with his family growing up when his father changed jobs yet again. Edouard Delaroche had tried everything from computer sales to being a barber and never stuck at anything for very long before getting bored. Musical theatre was hardly a stable profession, and sometimes Liam wondered if he'd chosen it partly for that reason. As the weeks slipped by in Cornwall, he found himself wanting to prove that he could do settled.

'Marlene's cake winning a prize in the garden show is very simple. The name of the show would be far too long if it covered all the various classes.' Ellie stirred the teapot and took two mismatched mugs out of the cupboard. 'A garden, cookery, needlework, art and craft show is a bit of a mouthful.'

'I guess so. It sounds a bit like the county and state fairs we have, although they've usually got farm animals and a fun fair as well.' Liam opened up the cake and cut two large slices.

'Oh, we have those too, but here they're separate events.' Ellie pointed to the cake. 'Find some plates and then sit down.'

'Yes, ma'am.'

She blushed. 'I'm such a school teacher, aren't I?'

'Yep, but there's nothing wrong with that.'

'Will used to say I was bossy.'

Liam took a few deep breaths. If he wasn't careful he'd tell Ellie exactly what he thought of her pompous ex-fiancé. The words pot, kettle and black came to mind. He caught her smile and guessed she'd read his mind again.

'Tea time, I think,' she firmly ended the not-quite conversation. 'Let's talk about your plans for Maria. Can she manage the stairs to get to your spare bedroom?'

'What choice have — '

'That wasn't the question I asked,' Ellie cut him off. 'You're worse than my five-year-olds.'

'Sorry.'

His sheepish expression made her smile. 'No, you're not. Put yourself in your aunt's place. She collapsed a few days ago and I'm sure her confidence is shaken. Your stairs are steep and very narrow.'

'What's your solution, clever lady? I'm sure you've got it all planned out.'

Ellie blushed. 'I did some thinking while I cleaned and it's really very obvious. When she was ill, Mrs Pascoe's son put a bed into the dining room but changed it again when they wanted to lease out the cottage. All you need to do is push the table up against the wall and put a single bed back in there. Move in one of the comfy chairs from your three-piece suite and maybe add a small

TV. You're lucky the Pascoes put a small shower into the hall toilet a couple of years ago, so that will be easy for Maria to use.'

Liam leaned across the table and gave her a loud smacking kiss on the lips. 'You're a genius.'

'You are a born flatterer.'

'Nope. I tell it like it is,' he declared. 'But how do I get it all done before tomorrow?'

Ellie frowned. 'I can't help until I finish work in the afternoon. I'm off school then for a couple of weeks.'

'I'm sure you have more interesting things planned.'

'I'm hoping to find a new flat but that's about it. It's time I got out from under everyone's feet.' Ellie wracked her brains. 'Ask Matt. I bet they've got a spare bed at the pub you could borrow. There aren't many visitors around yet, and won't be with the dreadful weather we've got forecast.'

'And you say you're not a genius.' Liam shook his head and laughed.

'After I've walked you home, I'll stop in the Red Lion and see if I can catch Matt behind the bar.'

Ellie gave him a hard stare. 'Why do I need walking home? I've walked all around Trelanow for nearly thirty years and survived unscathed. Amazing, isn't it?'

Liam's eyes narrowed. 'Sorry. I — '

'I don't blame you for being prickly.'

He gave a gentle smile and caressed her cheek. 'I *want* to walk you home. Is that a problem?'

'No,' she whispered, leaning into his warm touch.

'Good.'

They sat there in contented silence for several wonderful minutes.

'It's getting late,' Liam said.

'Mmm, I suppose it is.' Ellie couldn't bring herself to care. 'By the way, did you enjoy Marlene's cake?'

Liam's silvery eyes darkened. 'I sure did, but not enough to marry her.'

'Good.' They were on dangerous ground, but Ellie didn't seem able to stop taking just one more step, testing to see how far they could go. She tried to pull herself back to a more sensible place. 'I'll put the duster and Hoover away while you clear up our tea things.'

'Sure.'

His easy agreement didn't fool her for one moment. The school holidays were set to be a lot more eventful than she could ever have imagined, and the prospect set off a flutter of anxiety and excitement in the pit of her stomach.

17

'I suppose it'll have to do.' Maria sniffed and glanced around the temporary bedroom her nephew pulled together since yesterday. Ever since he had collected her from the hospital, she hadn't stopped complaining about everything from the small taxi and the narrow roads to the strict diet and exercise instructions she'd been given. Now she'd started on the cottage. 'Goodness knows how the people here manage. These tiny houses make me claustrophobic.'

'The longer I stay, the more I find I like it,' Liam ventured. 'It's simple and suits me. I suppose it wouldn't be so good if you were a family of six crammed in here.'

Maria gave him a searching look. 'You don't sound as if you're planning to return home anytime soon.'

'Home? I don't really have one.'

'Nonsense. New Orleans is your home.'

Liam shrugged. 'I guess, but I haven't spent much time there in years.'

'Whose fault is that?'

He kept silent, recalling his father's words just yesterday: *Treat your aunt kindly. I know she's not always been good to you, but she's my sister and your family when all is said and done.* It was a pity Maria and the rest of his family hadn't followed the same mantra when Liam needed support after Cathy's death.

'I'm dying for a decent cup of coffee,' Maria said.

'I'll fix us some.'

Maria grimaced. 'I suppose it'll be more of that decaf mud they forced me to drink in the hospital.'

'Yep, doctor's orders.'

'You're enjoying this, aren't you?'

You have to be kidding. If you think this is a barrel of laughs for either of us, you're nuts. 'Hardly.' The single dry word pulled the first hint of humour from his aunt's grim expression, and for a second he hoped she might actually break down and smile.

'Fine. Am I allowed anything to eat?'

'How about half a whole-grain bagel with a scrape of peanut butter?' He'd studied the diet sheet from the hospital and rung Ellie to discuss menu ideas before stocking up earlier.

'Wonderful. Bring it on.' She slumped in the chair and picked up the remote control, turning on the television and ignoring him.

It could be a long two hours before Ellie arrived to have dinner with them.

★　★　★

Ellie raised her hand to knock, but Liam flung open the door and pulled her inside. 'Boy, are you ever a sight for sore eyes.' He snatched the bowl of salad from her arms and set it down on the hall table before giving her a tight hug.

'That bad?'

He grimaced. 'Worse.'

'Maria's not happy?'

'Understatement of the century.'

'It that Ellie?' Maria shouted. 'Send her in here.'

'You heard the queen. Do as you're told.'

'She can wait a minute.' Ellie kissed him on the mouth, taking her sweet time and relishing every moment. 'That's better.'

'Sure is.'

'You got the bed okay?'

Liam nodded. 'Yeah, Matt was a great help. We got it set up this morning before the pub opened. He offered me a nightstand and lamp as well, plus a TV they weren't using.'

'Have you both forgotten I'm here?' Maria's demanding tone made them both smile, and Ellie pressed her face into Liam's warm chest to keep from giggling.

'That's not likely,' he muttered.

'We're coming,' Ellie called out, and reluctantly let go of Liam. 'Put the salad in the fridge and I'll beard the lioness in her den.' She straightened her shoulders and plastered on a smile.

'You're a star.'

'I'll make you pay. Don't worry.'

Liam chuckled. 'I'll buy you as many gammon steaks with the famous trimmings as you can eat.'

'You might regret making that offer. I've got a healthy appetite,' Ellie quipped, and hurried off before Liam could delay them any longer.

She pushed open the dining room door. 'Hello, Maria. How are you?'

'Dreadful.'

So pleased I asked.

'What dreary food have you got lined up for us? Liam tells me you're cooking.'

Until now, Ellie thought her day with twenty excited five-year-olds who couldn't wait to get out of school and whose minds were completely on Easter eggs was trying, but they'd been a cinch compared to this. No wonder Liam's patience was in shreds.

'I'm grilling salmon fillets with fresh herbs and a touch of olive oil, and serving them with a delicious kale salad and quinoa.' She used her best firm teacher's voice, the one that meant she didn't expect any more questions. A hint of respect shaded Maria's mutinous expression. 'Have you found something good to watch?' She gestured towards the TV.

'He doesn't have whatever your cable thing is called, so there are hardly any channels. It's like American TV about fifty years ago.'

'My mum and dad enjoy *Pointless*, the quiz show that's on BBC1 now. Maybe you could give it a try.' Again Ellie received a flash of something that could be perceived as admiration. This was the only way to treat the American lady. Any sign of weakness and she was doomed. 'I'll tell you when it's ready, and you can join us in the kitchen.'

'I'd prefer to eat in here.'

'Did the doctor say you couldn't walk that far?'

'No,' Maria grunted.

'In that case, I'm sure it'll do you good to move around.' Ellie softened her tone and rested her hand lightly on Maria's arm. 'You need to get your confidence back. I do understand. My father had a similar problem last year and it shook him for a while.'

'Is he fully recovered now?'

Ellie chose her response carefully. 'He's far more aware of his health these days and his doctor is very pleased with how he's doing. Dad will tell anyone who listens that it was the best thing that could've happened. Otherwise he'd simply have continued with his bad habits and probably had a far more serious stroke or heart attack that he might not have survived.' Maria paled under her make-up and Ellie wondered if she'd gone too far.

'You're not as sweet as you look, are you?'

Ellie was struck dumb by the blunt question.

'Off you go and get cooking. I'm

starving.' Maria waved her away.

In the kitchen Liam greeted her with a massive smile and an enthusiastic hug. 'That was brilliant.'

'You heard?'

'Yeah, I hovered close enough to listen. I wanted to make sure she didn't turn on you.'

Ellie frowned. 'You don't think I was too harsh?'

'Not at all. You only said what the doctor already told her and what I've tried to emphasise, but because you're you she listened.' He held up a wine bottle. 'Ready for a glass?'

'Definitely.' She laughed and got the salmon out of the fridge.

'What can I do to help?

'Top this up at regular intervals.' She grabbed the glass he held out and took a large gulp. 'You can find me a saucepan for the quinoa as well.'

'Yes, ma'am.' Liam chuckled. 'I'm not much of a cook, but I can follow instructions pretty well.'

It flitted through Ellie's mind that

this could do him good too. Anyone looking at Liam could see he wasn't eating properly. Maria wasn't the only one who needed to take care of herself.

'Don't your family mind you abandoning them?'

Ellie laughed. 'Hardly. It's one less body around the cramped kitchen table. Mum's changed a lot of her cooking habits since Dad was ill, and we can try some of her new recipes on your aunt.' Liam's dark eyes lingered on her and she swallowed hard. 'Is something up?'

'I'm simply wondering how I got lucky enough to meet you.'

'Oh.'

'It's okay.' He touched her burning cheek. 'No rush. No rush at all.'

But you'll go back to America soon, and then what?

'One step at a time. Isn't that how you teach little ones to read and write?'

Ellie nodded.

'Let's make a start by cooking together.' He brushed a soft kiss over her lips. 'You're in charge.'

One day she'd tell him how much she appreciated his casual assumption of being in this together, whatever 'this' was. For today it was enough. 'Why don't you fetch Maria while I get everything on the plates?' she asked.

Liam raised an eyebrow.

'It won't kill you,' Ellie whispered, not wanted his aunt to overhear. 'Offer her your arm to hold.'

'Fine.'

'And try smiling.' She laughed.

Liam grinned and sauntered out of the kitchen.

Ellie drained the rest of her wine and put the bottle back in the fridge just before they came back in.

'I could eat a horse,' Maria declared, sitting down with a loud sigh.

'That wasn't on the list of recommended foods. You'll have to make do with salmon,' Ellie teased.

'You Brits sure have a weird sense of humour,' Maria groused, but there was no real venom behind her words and all three of them burst out laughing.

Ellie caught Liam's eye and he couldn't hide his astonishment. She took a wild guess that it'd been a long time since he and his aunt had shared anything good. A warm feeling settled in her heart. Liam wasn't the only one who'd been lucky that day on the beach. She banished from her head the traitorous thought that luck could turn on the flip of a coin.

18

'Will you be all right if I leave a touch early for choir practice?' Liam asked. They were fitting a Good Friday practice in around the extra church services to be ready for Sunday. 'I want to warm up and run through my solo a couple of times before everyone gets there.'

'Stop fussing,' Maria insisted. 'I've got your odd little local newspaper to read, and Ellie will be here soon to have lunch with me.' She shooed him away. 'For heaven's sake, go and bask in the glow from your adoring fan club.'

A rush of embarrassment heated his face and neck. Ellie had amused his aunt last night by recounting the story of his karaoke performance and subsequent temporary role in the church choir. 'I'll be off.'

'Don't rush back. I've plenty to talk to Ellie about.'

Yeah, that's what worries me. 'All right. See you later.' Liam hurried back into the living room, dragged on his coat, and grabbed his music on the way out of the door. He fumbled in his pocket and pulled out an old black wool scarf to wrap around his throat.

He greeted several people as he walked through the village to the church, surprised by how many he knew after only a few weeks. Liam pushed on the ancient wooden door and it swung open to release the sound of the opening bars of Handel's *Messiah*. The organ music stirred his senses and he hummed under his breath. He wondered how he'd managed to live without his music for the last two years.

Harry stood near the front of the church, fiddling with a microphone stand, and gestured towards Liam to join him. 'Glad you came early, mate. The rest of them will trickle in soon, but a few are working today and can't make it.'

'I need to warm up before we start, and it takes me a good fifteen to twenty minutes.'

'Oh, right.' Harry sounded a bit bewildered.

'You stretch before doing any kind of sport, don't you?'

Harry laughed and patted his slight paunch. 'Do I look like a sportsman to you?'

'Maybe that wasn't a good analogy.'

'It's all right, I know what you mean. I suppose I'm used to dealing with people who amble into practice late, stub out a cigarette on the way in and have just wolfed down a full roast dinner.'

Liam struggled to smile while inwardly shuddering. He'd eaten his standard two poached eggs on wholegrain toast and a fruit salad made with chopped-up banana, apple and grapes. No dairy products and no citrus fruits. Only room-temperature water to drink.

'I'll leave you alone,' Harry said. 'You do your thing, and maybe we'll get started around eleven if we're lucky.'

'If you don't mind, I'll go over there where it's quiet.' Liam pointed to a small side chapel.

'Help yourself. I'll try to keep the women away.' Harry rolled his eyes.

'If they hear me doing weird stuff it might put them off.'

'I wouldn't bet on it.'

Liam smiled and left his friend to it. The old granite church was cold so he kept on his coat and scarf. He'd established his routine over the years and it never varied. First he did some gentle physical stretches to get his whole body loose before starting on his vocal exercises, slowly at first, and only going through one octave before gradually increasing his range. He used various humming and vowel sounds to open his throat so it wouldn't be strained when he started to sing.

Liam became aware of people moving around and chattering and guessed he'd better stop. He raised his hand when he spotted Patsy, and she hurried across to him.

'Are you free to go to the pub afterwards for lunch?' she asked. 'Ring Ellie and see if she can join us.'

'Um, I'm afraid she's stuck at the cottage with my aunt.' He quickly explained, and Patsy's bright green eyes gleamed.

'I'm sure she doesn't mind.' Patsy smirked. 'We could have a quick drink instead.'

'Maybe. By the way, Ellie said something about looking for a flat over the holidays. Are you two hoping to move in together again?'

'Afraid not.' Her smile faded. 'I'm not earning enough to be able to afford to move out, and my dad relies on me a lot more these days. He worked on the roads, paving and stuff, and it's wrecked his knees and back. He's on the waiting list to get his knees replaced but it'll probably be a while.'

'I'm really sorry.' Everyone had their burdens, and Ellie's friend harboured a heavy load under her constant smile. Liam really hoped she and Harry might find some happiness together. Over a few beers one night Harry had revealed some of his own story, not in a complaining way but simply stating facts. As the only son of older parents, he'd left Cornwall for university, but returned home straight afterwards and got a job at the local bank. He'd made his way up to manager while helping to take care of his ageing parents, and now it was only Harry and his mother left.

'It is what it is,' Patsy said. 'You know that.'

Liam stiffened. He wondered how much Ellie had told her friend about him.

'I'm not prying.' Patsy touched his arm. 'I'm normal and curious. I looked you up after our impromptu musical session.'

Liam glanced around at the rest of the choir and wondered how many of them knew about his background.

'Ellie says you got a raw deal.'

'And that's good enough for you?'

'Of course,' Patsy affirmed. 'Why wouldn't it be?'

'I don't know,' he mumbled. This wasn't the time or the place to delve any deeper.

'Come on, let's get started,' Harry shouted, clapping his hands. 'Stop all the noise and take your places.'

'We'd better do as we're told,' Patsy said.

'Yeah.' Liam decided to take a risk. 'He's a good man.'

She pinned him with her sharp eyes. 'And you're telling me that why?'

'No particular reason.'

'Right. Liar.' She laughed. 'You're no better than I am. There's a touch of the matchmaker lurking in you too.'

Liam shrugged. 'Time to go sing.'

★ ★ ★

'What did your fiancé do to make you leave him at the altar?' Maria asked casually, nibbling at one of the wheat crackers set on the table ready for their lunch.

Somehow Ellie held onto the tray she was carrying and only slopped a small amount of soup over the edges of the bowls. She made it to the kitchen table and quietly set one bowl in front of Maria before seeing to her own.

'What version of the story did you hear?' She kept her voice calm and steady, relieved to sit down before her knees gave way. 'And who from?'

'Don't worry, it wasn't Liam.' Maria gave a sly smile. 'The district nurse came in this morning to check on me. Nice little girl. Betty Grose, I believe she said her name was. Went to school with you.'

Ellie kept her expression bland and unreadable — at least, she hoped so, although her stomach roiled. Betty was no friend of hers and had always fancied her chances with Will. 'Oh yes, I know Betty.' If the nurse could say anything to put Ellie in a bad light, she'd do so with no qualms.

'According to her you, broke Will Burton's heart.' The plain implication behind the words was clear. *You do the same to my nephew and you'll be in big trouble.*

Maria didn't realise how much Liam

had already told Ellie about his fractured relationship with his family. His aunt playing the protective relative card wasn't going to work.

'I could say it's none of your business, but I won't,' Ellie said. Liam would smile to hear her now. 'Quite simply, Will and I had been together a very long time as friends and then more. Our lifestyles altered and we grew apart, but didn't acknowledge the fact and unwisely decided to marry. There were a lot of subjects we disagreed on that I don't intend going into. I should've spoken up before but I didn't. That's my only regret.' She picked up her spoon. 'I don't wish to discuss it anymore.' Maria's features hardened. 'Let's eat our soup while it's hot. It's a delicious three-bean and barley recipe my mum created.'

For a while they ate quietly in silence.

'I'm concerned for Liam — '

'I'm not discussing him either,' Ellie snapped, dropping her spoon with a clatter in the empty bowl.

'Oh well, if you aren't worried, I won't say another word.'

'Worried about what?' As soon as the question left Ellie's lips, she regretted it. The hint of satisfaction pulling at Maria's thin mouth made her itch to smack herself for being stupid. She'd fallen right into the other woman's trap.

'All this.' Maria gestured around the room. 'Liam is a talented man, and he's wasted here.'

'Who says so?'

'I can see why you might want to hold onto him. He's an intelligent good-looking man, and they're in short supply around here, but we both know he's made for better than this.'

Memories of Will flooded back. He'd put down Cornwall and declared Ellie to be a coward for not wanting to, as he put it, make a real life in London.

'He needs to go back home, reconcile with his family, and restart his career. It's been long enough now. People forget.'

That's where you're wrong. He

hasn't forgotten, and deals with it every day. Ellie's eyes prickled with tears but she refused to cry.

'You're a very stubborn girl.'

Ellie straightened her shoulders. 'Excuse me, but I'm thirty years old. I am not a girl. If we're talking about people being stubborn, you'd do well to look in the mirror.'

'Well, listen to you.' Maria's raspy laughter echoed around the room. 'I guess we'll see what happens when Liam's father arrives.'

'He's coming here? Does Liam know?'

'Not yet.' She smirked. 'Maybe I'll let you break the good news.' She yawned. 'I'm tired. I think I'll take a nap. Why don't you go and track down my errant nephew?' She leaned across the table. 'I'll be fine. Tell him I insisted.'

'All right. But I'd like to see you settled first.'

'Okay,' Maria conceded, and slowly stood up.

Ten minutes later Ellie stepped outside and gently closed the door behind her. Liam needed to know about his father, and she needed reassurance. What if Maria was right?

19

'Just one drink,' Harry pleaded as they left the church. 'You don't need to stay long, but I've got a proposition to put to you.'

'Okay, okay. Your girlfriend's had a go at me already. She suggested having lunch, and I said I had to get back to Ellie.'

'Girlfriend?'

Liam nodded at Patsy and quickly suppressed a smile as Harry stared resolutely down at the ground, his cheeks an unflattering bright scarlet. 'Come on. Let's go before you spontaneously combust.' He patted his friend's shoulder.

'Do you think that she thinks — '

'Don't ask me. Ask her.' Liam chuckled.

'I couldn't. I'm useless around women.'

'Not that useless. She's here, isn't she?'

'That's for the choir, not — '

Liam cut him off. 'Don't be dumb. Sure she likes singing, but Patsy didn't suddenly get a passion for being in the choir until you showed an interest in her. She's into you, pal.'

'Do you think so?' The amazement in Harry's voice would've amused Liam if it hadn't been borderline sad.

'I sure do. Come on, let's have that drink so I can get back and rescue Ellie.'

'Do I hear my name being taken in vain?' The soft scent of roses tickled Liam's nostrils and Ellie appeared by his side.

'Is Maria all right?'

'Yes, she's fine.' Ellie's clipped tone suggested otherwise but he didn't press. 'She's taking a nap and suggested I had a break.'

'You timed it perfectly. Harry talked me into having a quick pint at the Red Lion. He wants to pound my ears about something. Patsy's coming, isn't she, Harry?'

'I'll check.' Harry scurried away and left them alone.

'What's up?' Liam asked, knowing they wouldn't get long to talk.

'Nothing much.' Ellie shrugged. 'I can't tell you here. We'll talk later.' Her reticence bothered him. 'I promise it's nothing life-threatening.'

Over her shoulder he spotted Harry and Patsy heading back towards them. 'Okay. I'll hold you to that.'

'Hold me now,' she whispered, and Liam wrapped his arms around her, worried and frustrated because they couldn't sort things out right away. 'That's better.'

'Are you two going to stand there all day or are you coming for a drink?' Patsy challenged, flashing Harry an adoring smile. 'Lead the way, oh great choirmaster.'

'We're coming,' Liam and Ellie chimed in together, and the four of them laughed.

* * *

'There you go. A reward for all your hard work.' Harry set a pint of Tribute in front of Liam. 'Are you coming on Sunday?' he asked Ellie. 'This one is amazing.'

'He had most of us in tears.' Patsy shook her head. 'I've never heard anything like it.'

Liam's throat constricted. He'd received plenty of accolades over his career, but none had touched him this deeply. Ellie squeezed his hand but he still couldn't speak.

'I think I'll have to,' Ellie said. 'What are you singing? Not that it would mean anything to me,' she apologised.

'It's one of the common operatic tunes a lot of people recognise when they hear it,' Liam explained. 'I'm doing Cesar Frank's *Panis Angelicus*.' He brushed a soft kiss on her cheek. 'Don't worry, we won't expect you to join in.' For his cheek he received a sly dig in the ribs. 'So, Harry, what's rolling around in your devious brain now?'

Harry held up his hands. 'Me,

devious? Never.' His dark eyes gleamed. 'Did you notice two of the stained-glass windows were covered up?'

'Yeah, did they get broken?'

'Vandals. Little devils.' Harry shook his head. 'Cost a fortune to replace, and we've been raising money for a while but we've a long way to go.'

'Where do I come in?'

The other man went quiet and drank half of his beer in one swallow.

'Do you want me to ask him?' Patsy said, and carried on before Harry could answer. 'We wondered if you'd headline a concert to benefit the window fund. It'd take a lot of publicity to succeed, which you might hate, but maybe it'd be good for you to get back in the swing of things.'

'Can you give me some time to think about it?' he hedged.

'We could,' Harry answered, 'but it'd be great if the vicar could announce it on Sunday.'

Liam threw Ellie a pleading glance, but the blank expression on her face confused him. No sympathy. No enthusiasm for changing his mind. Nothing that gave him any clue as to how she felt about this wild idea.

Ellie ached to do or say something to help him out, but Maria's chiding words resonated in her head: *We both know he's made for better than this.* He was a grown man and must make his own decisions. She'd resented Will for trying to steer her down his chosen path instead of them choosing one together, and Ellie refused to do the same for Liam. This might only be a concert, but it meant encouraging him to stay longer in Cornwall, and could cause him untold anguish if the press latched onto it and dragged up his past.

'When were you thinking of holding this concert?' Liam ventured, and Ellie caught her friends giving each other a triumphant nod. 'Hey, I haven't said yes yet.'

'You haven't said no either,' Patsy retorted.

'We wondered about the first of

May,' Harry said. 'That's a Sunday, and the Monday is a bank holiday, which means if the weather's half-decent we should have a few visitors around. The ladies could put on a cream tea afterwards and make a bit more money that way. So are you in?'

Ellie's breath caught in her throat, and this time when Liam glanced her way she couldn't hold back a smile. The strain left his face and he reached for her hand, giving it a tight squeeze. At this moment she couldn't bring herself to care about Maria or common sense.

'I may live to regret this, but all right,' he conceded.

'This is so cool!' Patsy jumped up and threw her arms around Liam. 'You're the best.'

'Uh, yes, what she said,' Harry mumbled, regarding her friend with a sort of shell-shocked bemusement. 'Have you got time for another round? This calls for a celebration.'

'I suppose we could. Just a quick

one.' He glanced her way. 'Is that okay with you?'

'Of course.' She longed to get him on his own but couldn't spoil the moment.

'I'll give you a hand, Harry.' Liam offered and stood up. A slight frown creased his brow and he stared across the bar. 'I thought your brother and Will Burton didn't get on?'

'They don't. Why?'

'They're drinking together over near the pool table.'

'Snooker table,' Ellie automatically corrected him. 'We generally play snooker here, which is a nineteenth-century development of the much older game of billiards. Snooker got its name when an army officer stationed in India used the word to refer to another younger officer's poor play, 'snooker' being army slang for a new recruit. In America you developed a slightly different game from billiards and got the name 'pool' from the fact that players pot balls in a certain order to claim the collective stake or pool.'

The three all stared at her.

'It may be related in some obscure way to the French word *poule* for hen,' Ellie muttered.

'I'm sure it is, sweetheart.' Liam's eyes gleamed with good humour. 'Fount of all knowledge is my lady here.'

Her cheeks burned, and she wasn't sure if it was caused by his obvious amusement at her obsession with words or the way he'd casually called her his lady. 'To get back to the subject in hand,' she said, trying to collect herself, 'are you sure it's Grant?'

'Look for yourself.'

Ellie peered around Liam's shoulder and could hardly believe her eyes. Grant never had any time for Will, and the same was true in reverse, so why were they drinking together and deep in conversation?

'Wish you were a fly on the wall?' Liam asked. 'Do you want them to know we're here?'

'I don't think so.'

'Probably wise. It's always good to keep something up your sleeve in case you need it.'

'I'll help Harry,' Patsy offered. 'They won't pay any attention to how many drinks we're buying and wouldn't know who they're for anyway.'

'Thanks.' Liam sat back down and Ellie perched on the bench next to him. 'We've got a couple of minutes, so spill the beans on Maria. What did she say to rattle you?'

Ellie wondered where to start and how much to say.

'Come on, honey — everything,' he insisted. 'Don't worry, I know it won't be flattering. She might've mellowed a bit around you, but she hasn't to me.'

'Mellowed?' She winced. 'Not sure that's the right word. Biding her time is more like it.' A quirky smile lightened his serious expression. 'Five-year-olds aren't always innocent little cherubs, you know, and neither are their parents. I'm not naive.'

'Never said you were.' His eyes

sparkled. 'I wouldn't dare.'

'Good.' Ellie noticed Harry getting served and knew she needed to hurry up. 'Your father is coming.' Liam froze. 'Don't ask me when because she didn't say.'

'I don't know why she's making such a secret of it. They're very close and I thought he'd come to see how she's doing. What else?' he sighed.

'She had a go at me about abandoning Will at the altar.'

'How the heck did she find that out?'

Ellie shrugged. 'The district nurse who came to check on her knows me and . . . isn't a friend, shall we say.'

'I'm sorry. You shouldn't have to put up with that after all you've been doing to help.' Liam wrapped his arm around her shoulders and pulled her close, surrounding her with his intoxicating warmth. 'Something else?'

'Isn't that enough?'

'Sure it is, but that's not everything, is it?' he persisted.

Harry beamed and set down a tray of

drinks. 'Here we go. Let's drink to the success of our fundraising. Patsy's gone to the loo; she'll be back in a minute.'

Ellie picked up her glass of wine and immediately took a big gulp. She sensed Liam's simmering annoyance but couldn't bring herself to look at him.

Liam is a talented man and he's wasted here.

She'd hoped for reassurance, but that was the very last thing she'd got.

20

Liam adjusted his tie. Too tight and it would be uncomfortable for singing, but too loose and he'd look scruffy. He rechecked his phone for a message from Ellie but came up disappointed again. Yesterday she'd claimed to be busy, but he suspected she hadn't wanted to face him or his aunt. His plan to challenge Maria on Friday fizzled out because she'd still been asleep when he returned, her face sunken and grey, and looking every one of her sixty-five years. Later she'd plainly expected him to mention the conversation she'd had with Ellie, and it'd almost pleased Liam to disappoint her. If she didn't bring up the subject of his father's visit by tonight, he'd tackle her then.

'Are you sure you're well enough to come to church?' he asked.

'Of course I am,' Maria said, and

checked her watch. 'Ellie will be here in a few minutes to drive me over.'

'You've heard from her?'

'You haven't?' Satisfaction oozed through her voice and he struggled not to overreact.

'She's been busy.'

'I'm sure.' His aunt tugged on a pair of black gloves. 'This is the first Easter in forever I won't be digging into a good bowl of your father's gumbo followed by delicious honey-baked ham. I'll miss your mother's fresh coconut cake and boiled custard too.'

Liam didn't answer. She might not mean to be thoughtless but he couldn't be sure. The last time he spent Easter with his family was three years ago before he'd wrecked everything.

'Oh, well, let's go and see if you remember how to sing.'

A sudden loud knock stopped Liam from saying something he might regret. 'I'll let Ellie in.' He took a couple of moments in the hall to collect himself before opening the door. 'Wow, you look beautiful.' Ellie's bright yellow and green flowery dress shouted spring, and she'd scooped her beautiful hair into a ponytail tied with a matching yellow ribbon. The only concession she'd made to the appalling weather was by carrying an oversized see-through umbrella.

'Stupid, I know, but I was determined to wear it today.'

Liam ached to ask if she'd bought it specially but contented himself with leaning in close and brushing his lips over her soft perfumed cheek. 'I'm glad you did.'

'You look good too.' A pink blush crept up her neck and warmed her skin.

'It's a bit on the loose side.' Liam tugged at his suit jacket. 'But it fits better than it did. Must be all the pasties.'

'Don't forget the fish and chips.'

'How could I?' They smiled at the memory her words evoked.

'Are you going to ride with us?' Ellie asked.

'I will if you don't mind. I've done most of my warm-up exercises here, and being out in the cold and rain wouldn't be good for my throat.' Liam flushed. 'Sorry. That sounds fussy.'

'Don't apologise. You want to do your best. That's good.'

'What you really mean is I'm making progress.'

She smiled, not taking his wry comment the wrong way. 'Absolutely.' She nibbled at her lip. 'By the way, you were right.'

'How?'

'I didn't tell you everything on Friday,' she confessed. 'But I will later if you still want me to.'

'Deal.' Liam caressed her face, sliding his finger down to rest in the pulse at her slender throat. 'Later.'

'Are you two ready?' Maria stomped out into the hall.

Liam ignored his aunt's disapproving stare and gave Ellie a gentle kiss before letting go of her. 'We sure are. Let's go.'

* * *

The last otherworldly notes died away and Ellie breathed again.

'Now do you understand?' Maria whispered.

Ellie had known Liam was good, but not *that* good. But 'good' was a feeble word and didn't begin to encompass how amazing his voice truly was. Everything about him changed when he sang. He held himself differently, and when he finished his solo a peaceful expression settled on his face as though all was right with the world again.

'If you keep him from this, he'll come to resent you, and that'll poison whatever juvenile notion of love the pair of you think you have.' The woman's bitter words seeped into Ellie and she wished she had the nerve to tell Maria to shut up.

She forced her trembling hands to steady enough to pick up the service leaflet. Somehow she got through to the end. If she could talk to Liam now, maybe everything would be fine, but that was a hopeless wish because he was surrounded by people congratulating him. She spotted her mother heading their way.

'I'm Jennifer Teague, Ellie's mother. You must be Liam's Aunt Maria.' She plumped down on the empty seat next to them. 'You must be terribly proud of him. What a voice!'

Maria nodded and didn't say much, but that never hindered Jennifer, who rambled on and ended up inviting them all to lunch.

'I know you're on a heart healthy diet, but that's not a problem because so is my husband. We've got plenty of fresh vegetables and lean turkey, plus a delicious fresh fruit salad. You won't starve.'

'We couldn't poss — '

'Of course you can,' Jennifer stopped Maria's protest in an instant. Talk about two unstoppable forces colliding. Ellie smiled as her mother bulldozed through with a determination even Maria couldn't match. 'It's a steep walk up the hill but Ellie will give you a ride.'

'Thank you. You're very kind,' Maria conceded.

'It's wonderful of Liam to agree to do the concert for us. Everyone in the village is thrilled.'

Maria's tight smile betrayed her distaste.

'How are my favourite ladies?' Liam draped his arm around Ellie's shoulder and pressed a swift kiss on her forehead.

'We've been invited for lunch with the Teagues.' Maria's lack of enthusiasm was plain. 'I've accepted for us both.'

'Wonderful. Ms. Jennifer's a great cook. It'll be a lot better than the beans on toast I had planned,' he joked.

'Oh, you flatterer.' Jennifer poked his arm. 'Is he always such a charmer?'

'Not exactly,' Maria muttered.

Out of the corner of her eye, Ellie caught Will staring at her from across the aisle. She'd spotted him earlier leading in his parents, but carefully avoided looking his way all through the service. He gave a sharp nod and turned away, leaving her uneasy without really knowing why.

'It's okay. He's not going to bother you again,' Liam murmured.

I wouldn't be so sure. 'I had to park too far away for your aunt to walk, so I'll go and bring the car around outside the church gate.' She'd dropped Maria and Liam off earlier when all the closest parking spaces to the church were gone.

'I'll come with you.'

'There's no need.'

'Maybe not, but I'd prefer to.'

'Thanks,' Ellie conceded. 'We might have a hard time getting away from your fan club,' she teased.

'If we weren't in church, I'd — '

'Don't say it. You shouldn't even be thinking it.' Ellie grinned. 'Come on.'

They managed to escape, and as they stepped outside were both surprised to find the rain had finally stopped. The wet ground shone in the dappled sunshine and the swaths of bright daffodils lining the path fluttered in the breeze. Liam clasped Ellie's hand and his brilliant smile melted her heart. She pushed away their problems and simply enjoyed the moment.

Liam wasn't stupid. Something had happened in church beyond his singing. At a wild guess, he'd say Maria had stirred things up again with Ellie and put the frown back on her face.

'You'll come to the cottage tonight? Maria goes to sleep early. We can talk.'

'I suppose.'

'It's not an execution date.' He tried to keep it light.

'All right.' They reached the car and got in, driving back to the church in silence. 'You can fetch her.'

Liam nodded and clambered out. He strolled back into the church but ground to a halt inside the door. Maria and Will Burton were huddled together and absorbed in conversation. Liam's blood chilled as the words 'New Orleans' and 'family' drifted his way. Would he never get a break?

Harry appeared and slapped his shoulder. 'Well done, mate. That was epic. I'll be in touch tomorrow about getting a programme together for the concert.'

'Oh, yeah, sure.'

'Everything okay?' He glanced around. 'Where's Ellie?'

'She's waiting in the car. Her mother invited me and my aunt for lunch. What are your plans for the rest of the day?'

'I'm chief cook. Roast lamb.' Harry shifted from one foot to the other. 'Patsy and her father are joining us. It didn't seem to make sense for us to — '

'Hey, you don't have to justify yourself to me. I think it's cool and I'm glad you've got the ball rolling.' He glanced over to see Will had disappeared. 'I'd better go. Good luck with lunch.' Liam winked. 'If you're lucky, the parents will take an afternoon nap.' Harry spluttered and shook his head. 'I'm off.'

'Finally,' Maria griped as he got back to her. 'I thought you'd forgotten all about me.'

'You had company.' Two hot red

spots flushed her cheeks. 'Found plenty to talk about with Will Burton, did you?'

'Oh you know, this and that.'

'I'm sure.' Liam held out his arm. 'Ready to go?' She'd expected him to persist with his questions but he wouldn't. Not now. He'd save it for later. They'd have plenty to talk about then and all the time in the world to do it.

21

'Lover boy didn't get the hint, I see,' Grant said when he cornered Ellie in the kitchen. 'I thought you told him where to go.'

'Mind your own business or I'll set your wife on you,' she teased, but his stern expression didn't soften. 'I know your heart's in the right place, Grant, but you've got to back off.'

'He's not good enough for you, sis. I'm not a fan of Will, but at least he's a decent bloke.'

'I don't believe it.' Despite her frustration, Ellie still laughed. 'Only the other day you called him an idiot. Make up your mind.'

Grant shrugged. 'I might've misjudged.'

'Is it a case of the devil you know?'

'Ellie, is there any . . . sorry, didn't mean to interrupt,' Liam apologised, and turned to leave.

'You're not interrupting anything.' She touched his arm. 'Grant needs to take in another bottle of wine or Mum will come after him.'

Grant glared at them both, snatched a bottle of red wine from the counter, and slammed the door shut on his way out.

'What was all that about?' Liam asked. 'Let me take a stab. Me? I'm pretty sure he wasn't praising my singing this morning.' His wry remark made her angry. Angry that her brother wouldn't let go of his vendetta against this good man, and angry that Liam considered it normal for people to think badly of him.

'Don't let him spoil everything.' Ellie wrapped her arms around his neck and drew him to her. 'Please.'

Liam brushed a loose strand of hair away from her face and dragged a soft kiss over her cheek. 'The last thing I want is to cause trouble in your family, honey.'

'You may have to choose,' Ellie retorted. 'It might have to be that or give up our . . . whatever this is between us.' She ploughed on while she was still riled enough not to think things through too much. 'In case you have any doubts, *I* don't intend to give *you* up.'

A full-blown blush heated his face. 'Grant was right about something. I don't deserve you.'

'Maybe not, but you've got me.' Her confidence faltered. 'Unless you don't want me, that is . . . '

'Oh Ellie, trust me, that is not the issue here.' The ghost of a smile tugged at his mouth.

'Well that's a relief.' Her voice shook. The hubbub from the other room reminded her they weren't exactly alone. This wasn't the place for a heart-to-heart. 'What did you come in here for anyway?'

'Aunt Maria asked if there was more grilled asparagus and your mum sent me on a search.' He chuckled. 'I couldn't believe she was voluntarily asking for a green vegetable that's not deep-fried or cooked with pork fat.'

'We'll win her over yet and get her healthy.'

'I know we were going to talk later, but I need to clear the air with my aunt first. She won't like it.' Liam's expression darkened. 'I caught her chatting to Will after church today and I don't think they were simply wishing each other a happy Easter.'

'That's not in our favour.' Ellie frowned. 'Will can put a good spin on any story, which is why he's such a successful lawyer. He'll have made himself look good in her eyes.'

'I'd ask you to join us, but . . . I need to do this on my own.'

'I understand. The weather's not supposed to be too bad tomorrow. How about the three of us go for a drive along the coast? Maria might be more amiable out of the house.'

'I wouldn't bet on it,' he muttered under his breath. 'Are we ever going to have more than a few minutes on our own?'

Jennifer yelled her daughter's name from the other room and Ellie rolled her eyes. 'Not anytime soon, but tomorrow evening I promise we will.' She wriggled out of his arms and went over to the fridge to pull out a covered plate. 'Asparagus. Go and do your duty.'

'Yes, ma'am.'

For a second their gazes met, and a wonderful sliver of understanding passed between them.

* * *

Liam watched Ellie drive away from the cottage until her car disappeared from sight.

'You'll see her again in the morning. Stop moping like a lovesick teenager,' Maria ordered, and her attitude galvanised his determination to follow through on his promise to Ellie.

'We need to talk.'

'That sounds ominous. I assume you

aren't throwing me out?'

Liam remembered his father's warning and reined in his frustration. 'Of course not. Would you like a coffee?'

'Before you start in on me?'

Deflecting him with her typical aggressive defence wasn't going to work, but he'd let her get away with it for now. 'Coffee?'

'I suppose so,' Maria said with a shrug.

He escaped to the kitchen and took his time getting their drinks ready. Then he carried the two mugs into the living room and set one down on the table in front of her before choosing to sit alone by the window.

'What do you want to know first?' she asked. 'Will the fact that your father's arriving on Tuesday, and if the doctor agrees we'll travel back at the weekend, do?'

'Why make such a secret of it?'

A sly smile curved one side of her mouth. 'No reason.'

Everything you do is for a reason. You don't fool me.

'I suppose your sweet little girlfriend has been tattling,' she quickly carried on when he didn't respond. 'Yes, I admit I asked her why she jilted that nice young man. That's not a secret, is it?' Maria tossed back at him.

'No, but she was amazing and helped us a lot when you came out of the hospital. Did it ever occur to you to thank her instead of being unkind?' An angry flush lit up his aunt's face. 'What has Ellie ever done to cross you?'

'She's trying to ruin your life.'

'Ruin it?' He jumped to his feet. 'How dare *you* of all people accuse her of that! She's shone a light into places inside me that have been dark a long time.' Liam forced himself to sit back down. He must get back in control or he'd push his aunt into having another stroke. 'I want to know exactly what you said to her about my so-called great life.' If she truly knew him, Liam's quiet steady words would have warned Maria that his temper was teetering on a knife edge.

'I simply informed her that your

talents were wasted here and you'd end up resenting her if she lured you to stay.' She gave him an indulgent smile. 'I told her you need to go back home, reconcile with your family and restart your career.'

'How dare you,' he half-whispered, unable to believe what he was hearing. 'When or if I decide to do any of those things, it will be by my choice and no one else's.' No wonder Ellie had looked so forlorn and despondent on Friday.

'Your father agrees.'

'He can speak for himself when he gets here.' A nagging headache dragged at his temples. 'What were you saying to Will Burton this morning?' He might as well hear it all now they'd gone this far.

'Nothing much.'

'I'm waiting.'

'He asked a few questions about you and I answered them, that's all. Obviously he'd checked up on you — '

'Why obviously? He and Ellie split up months ago. It's none of his business.'

'Don't be an imbecile. Will Burton

isn't the sort of man to take being turned down lightly. He's determined to win Ellie back and is gathering all the information he can on you, his competition.'

Liam was insulted on Ellie's behalf. 'We're not two dogs fighting over a particularly juicy bone.'

'Just telling you like it is.' She tossed back the last of her coffee and gave him a shrewd stare. 'I'm not sure why I'm mentioning this, but I'd also watch out for Ellie's brother.'

'Grant?'

'Yep. I get the impression Will is taking advantage of Grant's protective nature to stir up trouble between the siblings.'

Liam tried to get his head around Maria's apparent change of heart. 'I don't get this. I thought you wanted to split me and Ellie up.'

'I do for your own good,' she hurried on before he could protest. 'But on your terms. I don't care for the implication that you aren't good enough for her.'

'You don't think it's got anything to do with the fact I barely escaped prison over my sister's death?' Maria's features tightened and he waited for the explosion. They could never mention Clare without coming to verbal blows. 'I'm sure Will brought that up.' His aunt nodded, and a rare glimpse of compassion lurked in her eyes. Liam went to sit next to her. 'I can't blame Grant. He may be heavy-handed, but if I'd have been as good a brother to my own sister . . . ' He dropped his head into his hands.

Maria rested her hand gently on his shoulder, and the simple touch eased his pain. 'Okay?' she murmured.

'Yeah. Thanks.'

'I didn't do anything.'

He jerked upright. 'It's the first time you haven't condemned me for failing Clare.'

'I loved her so much.' Maria's voice cracked and tears trickled down her plump cheeks. 'I've always been a real career woman, so it never bothered me when I didn't marry and I didn't want children. Except for — '

'Clare.'

'Yes.' She sighed. 'Clare was the prettiest baby and grew into a delightful child. Don't get me wrong, you and your brothers are all good boys, but something about Clare was special.' His aunt managed a weak smile. 'She's the only person apart from your father who ever loved me unconditionally.'

'I — '

'Don't lie, Liam. We've always struggled to get along.'

He sucked in a deep breath. 'We could try harder. I can't replace Clare, but maybe we can be on the same side for a change.'

Maria's gaze sharpened. 'If you really want this girl, we'll have to come up with a plan.'

'You'll help?'

'No one tells a Delaroche they aren't good enough for anything.'

Grant and Will didn't know what they'd unleashed. Liam smiled to himself.

22

Ellie reread Liam's text message and allowed herself a tiny smile. Maria hadn't turned into a fan of theirs, but she wasn't playing the wicked witch role anymore either.

Marc's shrill cry broke into her thoughts. With Grant on the night shift, she could help poor Tina and her plan at the same time. She tugged on her dressing gown and crept out of the bedroom and along the hall.

Ellie tapped on the door. 'Anything I can do?'

'Come in.' Tina's exasperation showed in her voice. 'Sorry if we woke you.'

'You didn't. I wasn't asleep.' Ellie held out her hands. 'Give him to me.' She took the wailing baby and walked around the room. Surprisingly, Marc went quiet and his warm, heavy body went limp in her arms.

'Goodness, you and Liam must be miracle workers.'

'He's far better than I am. This was sheer luck.' Over lunch today Liam had worked his genius again when no one else could settle the fractious baby, and spent ages holding Marc so everyone else could eat in peace. She glanced at her exhausted sister-in-law and couldn't bring up the subject of Grant's meddling. It would have to wait.

'What's up?' Tina asked, slumping down onto the bed and tucking a pillow behind her head. 'You've been preoccupied all day. Things are obviously good with Liam, so what's troubling you?'

'You're tired. Let me put Marc in his cot and you can get some sleep.'

'Ellie, don't avoid my question.' Tina's clipped tones made her smile. This was exactly how she kept Ellie's brother in line. 'Put Marc down and we'll go to your room to talk properly.'

'But he might — '

'Trust me, we'll hear if he wakes up again.'

Ellie couldn't argue with that. Truth be told, they'd probably hear Marc all the way down in the village. She settled the baby before following Tina.

'Right, tell me everything,' Tina ordered before curling up in Ellie's armchair and tugging a soft yellow blanket off the bed to wrap around herself.

Something about sitting in near darkness loosened Ellie's tongue and everything poured out: their problems with Maria, Will's persistence, and Grant. That was the trickiest part. 'I assume he told you about Liam's family and what happened to his sister?'

Tina nodded. 'I thought my dear husband had learnt his lesson when I told him to keep his nose out of it.' The steel returned to her voice. 'He should have.'

'I didn't want to say anything because I love Grant dearly, and you. I'm sure he means well, but . . . ' Ellie bit back a sob. 'I know Liam made a terrible mistake, and so does he, but I can't bear to see him hurt this way.'

'An older brother who's a policeman is probably the worst combination for a single girl to deal with,' Tina said, shaking her head.

'Did you know that Grant's been talking to Will?'

'Will Burton?' She made a face. 'When?'

'I was in the pub with Liam, Harry and Patsy on Friday lunchtime and we saw Will and Grant drinking together. Maybe Will's helping Grant with a case?'

Tina's scathing glance said what she thought of that ridiculous idea. 'We both know that's extremely unlikely. He told me he needed to go on shift early to cover for one of his mates.' She grimaced. 'Stupid man. Did he really think he'd get away with it? You can't sneeze in Trelanow without the news spreading that you've got the flu and don't have long to live.'

'True.' Ellie had to laugh. 'Will pumped Liam's aunt after church too. Anyone would think he was putting together a case against him.' She frowned. 'I wonder if that's what he's doing in his mind.'

'Could be. I hate you and Grant being at odds. Do you want me have another go at him?'

'Do you mind? I'm not a coward, but — '

'No one said you are, but I've got . . . ways.' Tina gave a coy smile. 'He's a very straightforward man and I know how to turn that to my advantage.'

Ellie held up her hands. 'Please. No details.' Both women broke into giggles. 'You're the best. Grant's a lucky man.'

'I totally agree.' Tina chuckled. 'I'll remind him of that fact.'

'I'll tackle Will.'

'Won't he go back to London tomorrow?' Tina asked. 'Maybe all this will quiet down when he's away from Cornwall and working again with other things to worry about.'

'I suppose that's possible.' Ellie hoped she wasn't seizing on that as an easy excuse to get out of facing her ex.

'I know you want this sorted, but perhaps it will be of its own accord.'

'I'll see what Liam thinks tomorrow.'

'Good idea. Sharing problems is always better than keeping things secret and working on them alone.' Tina grinned. 'You can ask your dear brother if that's true when I've finished with him.' She yawned. 'I'd better go to bed before I fall asleep here.'

'Thanks again. You've been ace.' Ellie held out a hand and helped her sister-in-law up. 'I hope my sweet nephew sleeps later than usual for your sake.'

'And everyone else's.' Tina's wry comment brought them both to laughing again. 'Good night. Or what's left of it, anyway.'

Left alone, Ellie crawled into bed and closed her eyes, desperate for sleep. Tomorrow promised to be a long day.

* * *

'Maria's not happy,' Liam confided as he opened the door to Ellie. 'She made me take her to Will's house this morning and was all set to give him a piece of her mind, but — '

'Don't tell me — he's left already to beat the traffic.'

'You're a mind reader.'

'No.' She slipped her arms around his waist and smiled up at him, immediately making his day better. 'But I grew up here and it's always the same. Anybody with any sense avoids driving to or from Cornwall at the busiest travelling times, and bank holiday weekends top the list. Even though the weather's been pretty lousy, we've still seen a fair number of visitors around, and most of them will be leaving today.'

'I'm afraid Maria wants to have a go at Grant next.' Liam shook his head. 'When she gets her teeth into something, she doesn't give up easily. You saw what she was like with me before this.' He attempted to smile. The truce he'd arrived at with his aunt was still so new he hadn't really got his head around the idea.

'Hard, isn't it?'

'Yeah,' he said with a weary sigh.

'If it's any consolation, I wanted to tackle Will too.' Ellie launched into a long story of how things went with Tina. 'Your favourite baby helped.'

'He's a good kid. Likes a bit of attention, that's all.' Liam grinned. 'Same as most of us.'

'You're right.' She glanced out of the kitchen window. 'We'd better hurry up and go before it starts raining again.'

'Excellent idea.' Maria appeared from the hall. He thought it'd been too good to be true — they'd actually had nearly five minutes on their own. 'We have some talking to do, young lady.' She held up a warning hand. 'I know we crossed swords the other day but things have changed.'

'Not everything.' Ellie let go of Liam and faced his aunt, calm as the proverbial cucumber. 'I won't be spoken to like a naughty child again.' He stared down at his feet and stifled a laugh, amused by the sight of the two strong women facing off. Ellie might be out-wardly sweet, but scratch the surface and a veritable tiger emerged.

Maria flushed. 'I'm sorry. I hope you'll accept my apology. I was out of line.'

Liam's jaw dropped. He wondered if that was the first time his aunt had spoken those particular words in decades, maybe ever.

'Of course. After all, in the end we both want the best for Liam, don't we?' Ellie's dulcet tones did nothing to cover up the determination etched into every inch of her beautiful face.

'We do indeed.'

Liam was pretty sure they'd be able to hear Maria's teeth grinding across the Atlantic Ocean in New York. 'Ready to go, ladies?'

'Falmouth, here we come,' Ellie declared. 'I've got a picnic in the car, and if the weather holds we'll eat it across from the castle overlooking the sea. The view's spectacular.'

'Perfect.' Liam's gaze met her's and

by the two heated spots on her cheeks he knew she'd read his mind again. The part where he talked about her being perfect too and tried to express how deeply he cared for her.

Tonight. If he didn't get her to himself for a while this evening, Liam thought he might go crazy.

*　　*　　*

'You've worn me out in a good way,' Maria said when they got back. 'If you don't mind, I'm going to have a quiet read in my room, and then it's an early night for me.'

Liam could have kissed her, but she'd think he'd gone completely around the bend instead of only half way there.

'I can see the attraction of this place more now.' She gave Ellie a shrewd stare. 'You're a smart girl . . . sorry, woman.' For some reason, the comment made both women laugh.

'I'd love to show you more of Corn-wall's beauty when you come back.'

Maria's eyebrows rose. 'You think I will?'

'Oh yes.' Ellie's assurance sent a frisson of happy anticipation coursing through Liam.

They all said goodnight, and when Maria's door closed Liam drew Ellie into his arms. 'Don't say anything for a minute. Let me hold you,' he pleaded.

'You won't get any argument from me.' She gave a satisfied sigh and settled into his embrace.

'Maria told me everything she said to you on Friday.'

'Everything?'

He tipped her chin to meet his gaze. 'Yeah. She was so out of line she was in another darn country, Ellie.'

'But — '

'But nothing.' Liam needed to make himself clear. 'I told her I make my own choices.' He brushed a kiss over her soft lips. 'I'd like to reconcile with my family; but as to restarting my career, that particular boat sailed a while ago.'

'You were amazing today. You can't

waste your talents. Maria was right.'

'Ah, Ellie, I loved singing again, but I want a much fuller life than travelling and performing all the time. I love teaching music, and I enjoy art too.' He blushed. 'I'll show you some of my charcoal drawings sometime. I've done a few since I've been here — the first for ages.' Liam prayed he wasn't being premature. 'I'm not asking for any sort of promise from you, but I'll lay this out there. I'm committed to being here at least another five weeks until the concert, and . . . I'm committed to you.' He caught her sharp intake of breath and was deeply afraid he'd scared her.

'Am I allowed to give you one in return even though you didn't ask?' Ellie's radiant smile shot straight to his heart. Somehow he managed to nod. 'Ditto.'

For a second it didn't click, and then Liam chuckled. 'For a lady who loves words, you sure don't waste any yourself.' He wrapped his arms back around her. 'That's enough talking.'

She didn't argue.

23

Ellie smiled and tucked the key into her handbag. This must be her year for snap decisions. Her mother would say she was mad, but she fell in love with the tiny cottage on first sight. Tucked away on a side street close to the harbour, she even had a prized sea view from her bedroom window and a tiny sun trap of a back garden. Luckily the owner's young daughter was in Ellie's class, and Mrs. Botallack had offered her a break on the rent to get someone reliable.

A flutter of anxiety settled in her stomach and she glanced at her watch. Liam was expecting her in a few minutes to meet his father and she wasn't looking forward to it. She turned the corner into Jetty Street and hesitated on the pavement outside Liam's cottage at the sound of raised voices drifting out through an open window.

'You were a stubborn little boy and you've grown into a stubborn man. Come home where you belong.'

Ellie gave a sharp knock before she could lose her nerve.

Liam flung the door open and yanked her inside. 'Thank heavens. My father's in fine form.'

'I heard.' She smiled. 'Open window. Loud voices.'

'Oh, great. I didn't realise we were entertaining the whole street.'

'Only me. It's quiet tonight.'

'Glad something is,' he groused. 'I guess you'd better come and get it over with.'

They stepped into the small living room and Ellie plastered on her brightest smile. It usually worked on small children and their parents, but the short, stocky man standing by the window simply gave her a long, hard stare. From the family photos she'd seen online, Liam took after his pale, slender Irish mother, and she spotted little in the way of any resemblance to his Creole father with his deeply tanned complexion and fierce dark brown eyes.

She strode across the room and stuck out her hand. 'Ellie Teague. It's a pleasure to meet you, Mr. Delaroche.' He grasped her hand and grunted something under his breath. 'I must thank you for bringing along the sunshine. Poor Liam was beginning to think Cornwall's always damp and chilly.'

'Not at all.' Liam came to stand by her and slipped his arm around her shoulder. 'It's always sunny when you're around.'

Ellie's cheeks flamed. 'He's such a flatterer. Did he get that from you?'

'Hardly,' Edouard Delaroche dismissed the idea, with no hint of amusement. 'My sister was right.'

'In what way?' Ellie ventured to ask, pretty certain it wouldn't be anything positive.

'She described you as a living, breathing Goo Goo Cluster.'

'What on earth is one of those?'

Now he cracked a smile, a perfect replica of Liam's familiar quirky one that crept up on her every time. 'It's an irresistible candy treat made in Nashville, Tennessee. They make it by combining marshmallow cream with nuts and smother it in chocolate. A perfect mixture of soft, sweet, hard and crunchy.'

She thought she'd been complimented but couldn't be sure.

'You won't mind me being frank?'

Ellie shook her head. 'Not at all.'

'I'm grateful for all the help you've given Maria while she's been sick, and my boy's looking better than he has in ages.'

'But?'

His shrewd eyes narrowed. 'You're not gonna make this easy, are you?'

'Why should she?' Liam interrupted, tightening his grip on her shoulder. 'Ellie's done nothing wrong.'

'Your father might disagree.' Her sharp comment hit home, and a flash of heat mottled Edouard's thick neck.

'I didn't mean to offend you,' he said.

'Oh yes, you most definitely did,' she countered.

'Edouard, I believe she's well and truly got your number.' Maria chuckled. 'You're a lousy liar.'

'I thought you were with me on this.' He grunted, plainly confused.

'I am . . . and I'm not.' Ellie and Liam exchanged a brief smile.

'Make your mind up,' Edouard said.

'Don't you be telling me what to do,' Maria snapped at her brother.

'I'm too tired for all this.' Edouard rubbed at his eyes. 'We'll talk more later. I'm gonna take a nap.' He glanced around. 'I presume you've got a bed for me somewhere in this doll house?'

'The spare bedroom's all yours,' Liam said. 'I'll carry your bags up.'

'Two hours. Be back here.' Edouard pointed at Ellie, and she wanted to tell him it was rude to point but restrained herself.

'She's not going anywhere,' Liam

retorted, his expression softening as he turned back to her. 'At least, I hope not.'

She shook her head, and a grin flickered on her face. With each day that went by, she found it harder to refuse him anything, no matter what layers of complication he added to her life.

* * *

'Wake me up at five.'

Liam clenched his jaw at the peremptory order. On the phone they'd put out feelers towards each other, but the moment his father stepped off the train they'd slipped right back into their old ways.

'Don't go for a minute. I've got somethin' for you.' His father dug around in his carry-on bag and pulled out a crumpled white envelope. 'From Edwin.'

Liam turned the envelope over in his fingers and made no move to open it.

'You won't find out what it says that way.'

'I can make a pretty darn good guess,' Liam said with a shrug. 'What *you* don't get is that it changes nothing.'

His father's face crumpled, and all the bluster he'd shown downstairs faded away. 'Cathy would hate us to be this way,' he growled. 'I'm sorrier than I can ever say. My only excuse is that her . . . going that way unhinged me.'

'Heck, *Popa*, it did that to me too.' For the first time in years, Liam used the old Creole name for 'father'.

'You're my eldest son. The day you were born, no man was ever prouder.' Edouard wiped at his tear-glazed eyes.

The reply Liam wanted to make stuck in his throat, but as he met his father's tortured gaze he knew he'd been understood anyway.

'Yeah, and I'm still proud, although you might not think so. You're a tougher man than me. I don't know how you've dragged yourself through this, but . . . I'm glad you have.' Edouard clasped

Liam's shoulder. 'Tell that pretty young lady I'll grovel to her later.' He managed to smile. 'She's quite a woman. You chose good, boy.'

Liam flushed with embarrassment.

'Don't fret, son. I know we men don't do the choosing.' A broad smile creased his father's face. 'If we're very lucky, we're the ones who get chosen. I remember that every day with your mother, and if I don't she's quick to remind me.' He chuckled. 'Get on with you and leave me to get some sleep before I drop on my feet.'

'Will do.' Liam knew he could say so much more, but for the first time in two years he had hope and for now that was enough.

Out on the landing, he hesitated and fingered the envelope flap. For two pins he'd throw it away unopened. He shoved the letter in his pocket and headed downstairs to find Ellie.

'I thought you'd got . . . ' Her smile disappeared along with her words. 'Is everything all right?'

'Yeah, I think it is.'

She raised an eyebrow but didn't say anything.

Liam glanced around. 'No Maria?'

'She followed your dad's lead and is taking a nap.'

'Seriously?' He couldn't believe his luck. 'Come here, gorgeous.' He flung his arms open and she nestled in with a happy sigh. For once he didn't have to worry about being interrupted and made the most of it, kissing her until she melted in his arms. Reluctantly he drew away. 'Worth waiting for.'

'Definitely,' she agreed, 'although I won't object when we don't *have* to wait, someday.' Two bright red spots coloured her cheeks, but he leaned back in and kissed her again.

'I'm totally good with that, honey.' Liam's heartfelt reply made her smile again. 'Let's sit down. I've got a ton of stuff to share with you.'

Her bright blue eyes shone. 'Sharing is good.'

'Sure is.' Liam gestured towards the

well-worn brown sofa. It had seen better days but would do the trick. 'We can cuddle at the same time.'

'Multi-tasking at its best,' she joked, and made a beeline for the sofa.

Liam settled next to Ellie and wrapped his arms around her, loving the way her silky hair rubbed against his neck, releasing the unique scent that was purely her. 'My father . . . we had a bit of a disagreement, but we hashed out things we should've sorted ages ago.'

'Perhaps now was the right time,' she suggested. 'Grief is different for everyone.'

'He gave me a letter from Cathy's husband.'

'What does it say?'

'I don't know,' Liam admitted and she shifted in his arms, the better to fix him with one of her stern teacher glares. Usually they were reserved for naughty five-year-olds, but occasionally she resorted to them for people like him. *Dumb idiots, you mean.* He let go of her and dug in his pocket. 'There you go.' He held out the envelope.

'Oh, no.' Ellie shook her head firmly. 'You must read it first. Then I will if you still want me to.'

'Fine.' Liam ripped open the flap and drew out the single sheet of paper. He scanned through Edwin's brief letter, his eyes misting over as he read the short to-the-point apology. Unable to speak, he thrust the letter at Ellie. 'Please.'

She read slowly and carefully, going through it twice before laying it down on the cushion next to her. 'He needs your forgiveness.'

Liam's father hadn't spelled out the obvious, but this brave woman had no hesitation. Could he live up to her faith in him? What would happen if he didn't?

24

Ellie wrapped her arms around herself, shivering in the cold bedroom. Today's grey sky, heavy with the promise of rain, coincided with her gloomy mood. If this was what the rest of the school holidays were going to be like, she couldn't wait for them to be over.

Had she been unreasonable? She'd run it around her head continually and changed her mind over and over again until she thought she'd go mad. *I'm not sure I can forgive him. This apology changes nothing.*

They hadn't even argued; it had been more a sense of resignation. Of not being on the same page.

'You're leaving?' Liam's incredulity had turned a knife in her heart, but she'd still walked out. She said she needed to think, and that things were moving too fast between them, but they both knew the truth. Ten long days and he hadn't tried to contact her. When she'd seen Matt behind the bar in the Red Lion, he'd made a point of telling her that Maria and Edouard had left last Friday after she'd got a clean bill of health from the doctor. Ellie had refused to be needled by his veiled questions about her relationship with Liam.

She looked around her new bedroom and briefly wished herself back home in Cliff Street. Several loud raps on the front door made her heart race. She took her time smoothing back her hair in the mirror and reapplying her lipstick before heading downstairs, where she glanced ruefully down at her paint-stained T-shirt and old jeans.

'Oh,' she breathed dejectedly when she saw who it was.

'Disappointed?' Grant leaned in to kiss her cheek and brought out a bottle of champagne from behind his back. 'House-warming gift.'

'How could I ever be disappointed by champagne?' Ellie declared with a cheeriness she didn't feel. 'Come in. You'll have to ignore the mess. Mrs. Botallack was happy for me to do any decorating I wanted and I've been painting the bathroom this morning.'

'I'll take a guess it's blue.' He touched a mark on her chin and laughed. 'Let's hope your painting's better than your singing, sis.'

She wanted to join in the joke, but one mention of singing and everything slammed back. The huge gaping hole left by Liam ached as if she'd been kicked in the stomach.

'Sorry. Tina says I'm a typical flat-footed policeman, and she's right.'

'Your wife's a smart lady. You should listen to her more.'

'I know.' Grant shoved his hands in his pockets and couldn't quite look at her. 'Will tried to pull one over on me. He's slick.'

Ellie wasn't about to make this easy for him. She'd had enough of being treated like a child who didn't know her own mind.

'He said it'd be my fault if anything happened to you because of your 'association' with Liam.' Grant's bitterness seeped through. 'Will wanted me to join with him to make it impossible for Liam to stay in Cornwall.'

'But how? His sister's death is old news and not exactly a secret.'

'Yes, but if it's spread around again the right way it'll be impossible for him to star in a concert supported by the church, and Will believes the embarrassment will drive him away.' He rested his hands on Ellie's shoulders. 'I told him I wanted nothing to do with it, but — '

'You think he'll do it anyway?'

Grant gave a slight shrug. 'He's not a man who likes to be crossed.'

'Surely he can't think this will send me running back to him?' None of this made sense to her. She thought she'd made herself perfectly clear.

'He's got tunnel vision where you're concerned.'

'What can I do to stop him?'

'Tell Liam everything. He needs to know what's in the air.'

Ellie didn't want to admit that they weren't even talking at the moment.

'My smart wife was right again, wasn't she?' Grant shook his head. 'You've split up. What happened? Come home with me. I'm sure Mum can stretch the stew a bit further,' he pleaded.

'Thanks, but I honestly can't face everyone tonight. Stay and have a quick cup of tea with me and I'll tell all.' Ellie tried to sound flippant but failed, judging by the sympathy etched deeply in her brother's face.

'Okay.'

Ten minutes later, Grant had winkled far more out of her than she'd intended to say. No wonder he was good at his job. Ellie had heard from some of his colleagues that if there was a particularly difficult suspect who was resisting questioning, they always called in her brother.

'Couldn't you have cut him some

slack? You put the poor bloke on the spot.'

Ellie would have burst out laughing if she wasn't a hair's breadth from crying. 'You've changed your tune.'

'You know I'm right,' Grant insisted. 'I've got to go.' He put his tea mug in the sink. 'Think about it.'

When she didn't answer, he left; and as the front door closed behind him, Ellie lowered her head to the table and wept. For her stupidity. For the love she'd recklessly thrown away. And for poor Liam who'd done nothing to deserve her disdain except be honest with her.

* * *

Liam decided life was a seesaw. Just as he managed to get one side balanced, the other shot up into the air and then smacked him down hard. Things were better with his family than they'd been in several years, and he'd actually been sorry to see his father and aunt leave.

244

He'd even picked up the phone last night and spoken to Edwin for the first time since the blazing row they'd had after the acquittal. Liam had decided to go home and make his peace in person soon — maybe sooner than he'd intended, unless things changed drastically.

The concert plans were coming together, and he'd spent several productive evenings with Harry and the choir helping to train them to accompany him on several of the songs. It did his heart good to see his new friend happy with Patsy, if still a little stunned as to how he'd managed to acquire a beautiful girlfriend without any huge effort on his part. They fitted his father's 'choosing' theory perfectly.

But then there was Ellie — or rather, there *wasn't* Ellie. He'd spotted her around the village several times, and once she'd stared right at him, her eyes wide with panic, before hurrying away in the opposite direction. Heartsick and disappointed was the closest he could come to describing the hollowness inside him. He'd fully expected her to come to see him the next day and say she'd been too hasty. Then he would have told her he'd reached out to Edwin and things were good between them. But she hadn't given him the chance, and he'd been too stubborn to make the first move.

He checked the time and realised he ought to go. He had promised Matt he'd stop by for a drink and learn how to play darts. Anything was better than another evening on his own spent staring vacantly at the television and drinking too much coffee. For early April, there was still a distinct chill in the air, so he unhooked his old black coat and shrugged it on, then buried his nose in the collar where Ellie's perfume still lingered in exactly the way she'd seeped into every aspect of his life. He almost took the coat off again; but if this was his only contact left with her, he couldn't give it up.

Pull yourself together.

The moment Liam stepped outside, the gusting wind swept up around from the harbour and stung his face. He tugged his collar up and turned back to lock the door.

'Can I have a word?' Grant Teague appeared from nowhere, and if it hadn't been for the diffident expression on his face Liam would've been tempted to tell him where to go.

'Why? Come to rub it in, have you?'

'You fancy a drink?'

'I guess.' Liam shrugged. 'I was heading to the Red Lion anyway.'

They walked along together, neither one talking, and Liam's mind raced through the possible reasons for this unexpected visit. Inside the pub, he glanced towards Ellie's favourite corner, both relieved and disappointed not to see her there.

'I'll get them in. Pint of Tribute?' Grant offered.

'That'll work,' Liam said, catching Matt's eye behind the bar. 'I won't be long. We're still on.' He wanted to make it clear to Ellie's brother that he wasn't

247

in the mood to pretend to socialise.

Matt opened his mouth to say something but then changed his mind. There was an empty table by the window, and Liam hurried across to snag it before anyone else had the same idea.

'Here we go.' Grant passed a drink over to him and settled down with his own. 'I won't waste your time. You know why I had a go at you in the first place.' He gave a dismissive shrug. 'Not apologising for that.'

'Wouldn't expect you to. So what're we doin' here?'

A flush of heat raced up Grant's neck. 'I got something today you need to see.' He pulled a wad of paper from his jacket pocket. 'This is all Will Burton's doing. I, uh . . . he wanted me to be a part of it, but I refused and told him to leave it alone.'

Liam held out his hand but Grant made no move to pass it over.

'These posters are plastered up all around the village, and he claims he's sent copies to the local papers and directly to the church.'

'Do I get to read it or are you gonna keep me guessing?'

Grant flattened out the small poster, and for a moment all Liam saw was Cathy's smiling face. Gingerly he picked it up and struggled to focus on the words. It brutally condemned him and asked how the village church could consider him a suitable person to be involved with its fundraising. He grimaced. 'I'd say he hates me, wouldn't you?'

'We can't charge him with anything, I'm afraid.'

'Yeah, well, it's all true.' Why had he been stupid enough to think he could start over again here?

'Surely Harry knows?' Grant asked, and the compassion in his voice startled Liam.

'Yes, but he didn't broadcast it.'

A gleam brightened the other man's eyes. 'Maybe that's exactly what he needs to do.'

'What are you getting at?' Liam

didn't ask why Grant cared one way or the other.

'Can you trust me to talk to Harry?'

None of this mattered without Ellie, but Liam struggled to drag out the approximation of a grateful smile. 'Knock yourself out.'

Grant drained his glass and pushed back his chair. 'Don't give up yet.' He jumped to his feet. 'She's miserable too, you know.'

'I'm sorry.'

'Number Three Town Street. Ellie moved in last week.'

'Let me get this right.' He couldn't get his head around this. 'Are you telling me to go see her?'

'Your choice, mate.'

Choice. There was that word again.

'She might throw you out on your ear. My sister's a feisty woman when she's roused.'

Tell me about it. 'I'll think on it.'

Grant grinned. 'Don't take too long. I'm off. I'll be in touch.'

'Okay . . . and thanks.'

'No problem.'

Left alone, Liam slowly sipped his beer.

'Ready for your darts lesson?' Matt stood in front of him and Liam guessed his friend had seen the ubiquitous posters.

'Not tonight, pal. Got something I need to do.' *Something I should've done days ago.*

25

The wind whipped Ellie's hair around her face, and she could barely see for the tears coursing down her cheeks. She tugged at the revolting poster, but her hands were frozen and she only succeeded in ripping one corner.

'Leave it.' Liam's raspy voice startled her and he grasped her hands, wrapping them with his warmer ones and rubbing the circulation back to life. 'I've just been to Town Street but you weren't there.'

'Why?'

'Why was I there, or why weren't you?' His quirky smile unravelled the threads caging her heart that had prevented it from feeling anything but a dull, sad loneliness. 'You weren't there because you were here, and I was there because I came to see you.' His eyes turned slate-grey in the early-evening shadows. 'I've been an idiot.'

'I was the idiot,' Ellie protested.

He wiped away her tears and pressed a soft kiss on her mouth. 'How about we agree we were both less than smart?'

'Works for me.' Her voice wobbled. 'Have you seen these awful things?' She gestured towards the bedraggled poster.

'Yep. Your brother came to tell me all about them and offered to help sort it out.'

'Grant did?'

'Yeah, it surprised me too,' Liam admitted. 'He's not a bad guy. He can't help wanting to look out for you.'

'I know.' Ellie smiled. 'Tina had a go at him.'

'Thought so.'

'Do you want to see my new abode?' she asked, and the first sliver of happiness she'd felt in ages burst through before she remembered why she'd been out in the first place.

'Don't fret about it now, sweetheart,' Liam pleaded. 'Make me tea. Force-feed me with cake. Anything. Nothing is more important than sorting things out between us.'

Ellie longed to ask how he could be so seemingly unconcerned; but from their first meeting on the beach when Liam drew her in, and after ten lonely days, all she wanted was to bask in his company again. 'You're right.'

A mischievous grin lit up his face. 'Bet I won't hear that very often.'

'Make the most of it.' She linked her arm through his. 'Come on. Let's get in out of this wind. So much for spring time.'

*   *   *

'It's neat. You've made it yours already,' Liam said as he joined Ellie in the tiny kitchen after having a look around downstairs. He leaned against the counter and wondered where to start. He supposed that where they'd left off was good a place as any. 'I phoned Edwin and we had a good chat. He completely agreed with the story Cathy told me and knew how persuasive she could be. It doesn't let me off for being dumb enough to go along with her, but nothing could.' He gave a wry smile. 'I'm not sure Edwin and I will ever be best buddies, but that's okay.'

Ellie nodded, dropping a couple of tea bags into a large brown china teapot and pouring on the boiling water. She gave it all a good stir before putting on the lid and covering the pot with what looked to Liam like a bright green frog-shaped pillow. She noticed him staring. 'Haven't you seen a tea cosy before?'

'I didn't know teapots needed to be kept cosy. Do they catch a cold or something?'

She snorted. 'Don't be silly.'

Liam wasn't idiotic enough to say she was the one wrapping up her china to keep it warm.

'While it steeps you can tell me how Maria's doing. Matt told me she and your father returned to America.'

This was safer ground, and he told

her everything, including the fact that he'd be going back for a visit fairly soon to reconnect with the rest of his family.

'Oh Liam, I'm so pleased.' The tears glistening in Ellie's eyes made his throat tighten, and for a few seconds he couldn't speak. 'I know you don't want me to apologise, but I'm going to anyway. Trying to bully you into forgiving Edwin was beyond thoughtless. Nobody can order another person to do anything like that — it's got to come from the heart when the time is right.'

'You're too hard on yourself,' he protested.

'No, I'm not, and don't you dare trot out the worn out phrase about me meaning well.'

'But you did.'

'Maybe, but it's no excuse.' An impish smile brightened her beautiful face. 'Let me beat up on myself, please. It'll make me feel better.'

Liam held up his hands. 'Okay, I give in.' He noticed her thoughtful look. 'Spit it out.'

'What?'

'Whatever's still bothering you.'

Ellie blushed. 'I shouldn't say this. We're not . . . I mean . . . '

'You can ask me anything. Anything.' Liam caressed her cheek. 'Don't hold back, honey, please.'

'You talked about visiting your family.' She tripped over her words. 'The word 'visit' sounds as though you're not returning there to live anytime soon. Are you planning to stay in Cornwall? I mean, sort of . . . long term.'

'Would that idea please you?' he whispered against her soft, warm skin. His heart soared when she nodded, gazing at him with big blue eyes full of what he hoped were happy tears. 'Don't say I'm crazy, but I love you and I can't imagine my life without you in it.'

'If you're crazy, then I am too,' Ellie confessed. She did the hesitating, thoughtful thing again, and he took a wild guess this time.

'I know it's quick, and I'm not pushing. Getting to know each other better needs to be top of our agenda.' He flashed a grin. 'Of course, we might need a few more kisses to help the process.'

'Only 'might' and 'a few'?' She pouted, but the twinkle in her eyes gave her away.

He laughed and lowered his mouth to hers, dragging them into a deep and wonderful kiss and pushing everything else away in the best possible style.

★　★　★

Ellie was startled by the loud rap on the door. 'Are you expecting anybody?' Liam murmured, absentmindedly stroking her hair. He'd loosened it from its normal sensible braid as they lay together on the sofa, and the only light in the small room came from the flicker of the electric fire.

'No,' she said.

'It's only me,' Grant shouted.

Ellie reluctantly got up. 'I'm coming.' She fumbled with the lock. 'What do you want?'

'Charming, I'm sure.' He pushed past without waiting to be invited in. 'Oh, sorry, Liam. Good to see you here, mate.'

Mate? Had her brother been replaced by an alien?

'I can kill two birds with one stone now.' Grant gestured towards Liam. 'I was heading your way next.'

'Do you want to sit down?' Ellie supposed she ought to be a bit more welcoming, because he'd apparently encouraged Liam to come and see her in the first place.

'Can't stop.' He shoved his hands in his pockets. 'Tomorrow evening. Six o'clock in the church. Special meeting.'

'Choir practice?' Liam asked. 'Harry didn't mention one, and why . . . ' His voice trailed away. 'Oh.'

Ellie perched on the arm of the sofa next to him, putting her arm around his shoulder.

'It's open to everyone.' Grant half-smiled. 'Even tone-deaf people like my dear sister.'

'There's no need for all this.' Liam

exhaled a heavy sigh. 'I'll quit and make it easy for everyone.' He struggled to his feet and thrust out his hand to Grant. 'Thanks for trying, but I'm not putting Ellie through any more embarrassment.'

'You are *not* embarrassing me,' she insisted. 'It's my useless ex-fiancé who doesn't know when to stop crashing into a brick wall. I'll sort him out, and — '

'Cool it, sis,' Grant murmured. 'You too, Liam. Don't jump to conclusions, either of you.'

'What do you mean?' Ellie persisted.

He drew a finger across his throat. 'I'm sworn to secrecy. Just be there. Okay?'

'Fine,' Liam muttered.

Grant said goodnight and left, closing the door behind him. Neither of them spoke for a minute, until Ellie couldn't keep her curiosity in check any longer. 'What do you think — '

'I don't,' he interrupted, 'and I'm not going to. We'll wait to see what happens tomorrow.' His dark, smouldering gaze rested on her. 'Trust your brother. He's on our side.'

Ellie yearned to believe him.

'We're gonna sit back down, and you can tell me your plans for this place.' Liam's forced smile didn't fool her, but she'd try to play along. 'I'm not bad with a paintbrush.'

Her throat tightened. That was his way of telling her he wasn't going anywhere.

26

Liam tightened his grip on Ellie's hand as they stepped inside the packed church. A hush fell as people spotted them, although he noticed a few muttered asides and the occasional finger pointed in their direction. He ground to a halt at the sight of Harry and the vicar standing together at the front with Will Burton, slick as ever in one of his smart London suits and glowering straight at him. Somehow he managed to keep walking, pretty sure it was only because of the woman glued to his side.

Harry raised his hand for people to be quiet. 'We asked you here tonight — '

'Stop. Please.' Liam struggled to steady his voice. 'I'm grateful for everything you've done, but Will was right.' He shrugged. 'His motives were . . . suspect, but that doesn't change the truth.'

'Finally someone around here has

some sense,' Will growled.

'Y'all don't want me humiliating the village, and I don't blame you.'

Ellie's eyes blazed. 'That's ridiculous.'

'Please, love, don't.' Liam squeezed her hand. He ached to convey to her that none of this mattered. As long as she was on his side, he could let the rest go. Letting people down didn't sit easy with him, but there was little he could do about it.

A wry smile crept over Harry's face. 'You daft so-and-so. Did you really think we got all this together to publicly dump you from the concert?'

'We're supposed to be taking a vote on kicking Delaroche out,' Will protested. 'It's why I raced down from London and you know it.'

'Be quiet and listen for once,' Harry snapped. 'When everybody saw those disgusting posters of yours, do you know what happened?' He didn't wait for a response. 'People ripped them down. They complained to the police.

Then they came to see me and the vicar.'

Liam stood spellbound, listening to his usually quiet friend with newfound awe.

'They weren't having you sticking your oar in about who they could or couldn't have sing here.' Harry chuckled. 'There were a lot of, um, shall we say uncharitable suggestions as to what we should do with you.'

'But — '

'But nothing.'

'I caused my sister's death,' Liam forced the words out. 'There's no getting away from that.'

Harry grasped his arm. 'Everyone here reckons you've paid for your mistake. You're still paying, aren't you? Always will be.'

Liam blinked back tears, determined not to break down.

'It's not our right to put the boot in and kick you again.'

Liam didn't have a clue what he'd done to deserve this, but these people had taken him into their hearts and welcomed him. He would never be able to repay their generous trust.

'You don't really want to quit, do you?'

'No.' Liam's voice cracked.

'Good.' Harry beamed at the assembled crowd. 'We'll make this the best concert ever; and if we don't raise enough money to replace those windows, I'll — '

' — shave off your beard!' Patsy shouted from the choir, and a ripple of laughter spread around the church.

'She hates it,' Ellie whispered. 'My guess is he'll get rid of it for her either way.'

'He will if he's smart,' Liam agreed, knowing he'd do anything his Ellie asked.

'Right, that's enough drama for one night,' Harry declared. 'I suggest we all go for a drink.' He wagged his finger towards Liam and the rest of the choir. 'Not too many for you lot. We've got practice tomorrow morning at nine o'clock before the usual service.'

'Are you serious?' Will exploded. 'You're letting this . . . this no-good — '

Grant stepped out of the crowd, his expression stern and unyielding, arms folded across his broad chest and looking every inch the policeman. 'Take my advice and leave. Now.'

'You can't make me.' Will's petulance drew a round of titters from the people close enough to hear.

'Will, just go,' Ellie pleaded. 'Don't do this. It's over.' Liam caught her eye and knew she was referring to a lot more than the other man's abortive attempt to stop the concert.

'You're making a big mistake.' Will reached out to touch her arm but she stepped away. He shook his head and strode off, pushing people out of the way in his hurry to leave.

Ellie beamed at Liam and couldn't suppress her obvious happiness.

'I think me and your brother could get to be friends,' he mused. 'Come on, let's hit the Red Lion.'

The meeting started to break up, and

Liam made his way around the church to thank as many people as he could. Eventually it was only the Four Musketeers left. 'Anyone for karaoke?' he invited. 'It's Saturday night.'

Harry, Patsy and Ellie rounded on him with distinctly unfriendly glares, and he decided keeping his mouth shut for now might be his best move.

27

The last three weeks had flown by, and sometimes Ellie needed to pinch herself. If she hadn't gone for a rainy-day walk on the beach, would she be here today?

'Does this look okay?' Liam frowned and adjusted his bow tie in the mirror before turning around.

She longed to tell him how handsome and out of her league he appeared today, but he'd laugh and tell her not to be ridiculous. The immaculate black tuxedo, paired with a crisp white shirt and black patent shoes, combined with a fresh cropped haircut and perfect shave, all changed him. Ellie supposed she should prefer him smartened up, but missed his usual more laid-back style.

'I'll take your silence as a yes.' His dark smoky eyes rested on her. 'Don't fret; I'll be back to jeans and T-shirts in a couple of hours.' Somehow he always knew how to calm her unease. They'd had plenty of those moments but always got through them. 'You coming with me while I warm up?'

'If you want.'

'I want very much.'

'And I suppose stars always get their every wish granted?' Ellie teased.

'They do if they're very lucky.' Liam slipped his hands around her waist and drew her to him for a long, wonderful kiss. 'I'm one lucky man and I will never ever forget it.' His fervency brought a rush of heat to her face.

'We're both lucky,' she agreed. Ellie struggled to focus on something apart from his intense gaze, but it was almost impossible. 'Are you going to tell Maria and your father that we're leaving?' she croaked. They'd arrived from London yesterday in time for today's concert, and it felt right that they were here to share this moment.

'There's no need. They plan on

walking over to the church later. I'm amazed to see how seriously my aunt is taking the doctor's diet and exercise recommendations these days.' He touched her hair, loose around her shoulders today at his request. 'Thanks. You spoil me.'

Ellie laughed. 'Oh, and you don't do the same in return?' She'd never known anyone so generous of spirit. It didn't matter if it was giving her a foot rub after a long day at school, or free voice lessons to several local children who had talent but little money to spare — nothing was too much trouble.

'Come on, woman, or I'll be late.' He seized her hand.

They walked to the church in companionable silence because Ellie knew Liam preferred to rest his voice before singing. She'd cooked him his requested two poached eggs on wholegrain toast a couple of hours ago and tucked a bottle of room-temperature water into her handbag for him. 'I'll find a good seat and see you later,' she said as they went in.

'Break a leg,' she joked. He'd instructed her not to wish him good luck because it would jinx him. Of course she'd rattled off the possible etymology behind the words as being from an ancient Yiddish phrase translated into German. That'd only made him laugh harder.

Liam sneaked a quick kiss and left her, walking over to join Harry, who was talking with the pianist.

Going through the same rituals calmed his nerves, and once he'd completed his preparation Liam kept to himself while the church began to fill up. They'd sold out every ticket, and if some people were coming simply out of curiosity he didn't care. With Harry he'd decided on a wide variety of music to hopefully appeal to all tastes. Most he'd perform as solos, but a few would be with the choir. They were doing everything from opera to classic Broadway favourites, with a few unique versions of modern pop songs thrown in for good measure.

Harry touched his shoulder. 'Ready, mate?'

'Yep. Let's do this.'

His friend's expression turned serious. 'Who would've thought it? Fish and chips and karaoke.'

A lot had happened since then, and the other man wasn't simply talking about the concert. Liam wasn't the only one whose life had turned around. 'Worked for us, didn't it?'

Harry nodded. 'Did I tell you my mum's decided to move in with her sister at Mousehole?'

'No. That's good, right?'

'Certainly is,' Harry said, blushing furiously. 'Patsy's father got the word from the hospital to go in next week to have his knees done. Once he's recovered, we reckon he'll be all right living on his own if she pops in most days. I mean . . . well, you know what I'm getting at.'

Liam grinned. 'Oh yeah. Only hope you make a better job of it when you propose.'

'Propose?' Harry's voice rose.

'That's what you meant, right?'

He shuffled awkwardly. 'Well yes, but . . . what about you and Ellie? I'm not the only one with plans, am I?'

Liam's cheeks burned. 'No. She's agreed to come to New Orleans with me in the summer to see my family on their home turf. After that . . . ' He shrugged, unwilling to put it into words yet.

'We'll get there,' Harry assured him. 'Come on, let's sing us some new windows.'

Liam nodded and stood by the side door to wait for his introduction.

The next hour flew by, and considering how out of practice he was, things didn't go badly. He'd spotted Ellie, Maria and his father in tears when he sang the *Panus Angelicus* again, and they weren't the only ones in the audience wiping their eyes. Having that effect on people always awed Liam. He proceeded to send them on a roller-coaster ride by switching things up with their old karaoke favourite *Summer Nights*, taking off his jacket and managing a passable John Travolta impression with the help of Patsy. She'd turned into a decent singer, and Liam got a kick from seeing the admiration in Harry's eyes.

He ended up by singing *Ave Maria* unaccompanied, always guaranteed to silence an audience. It did the trick, and it took a few seconds for them to gather themselves and start their applause. Liam barely heard the vicar's speech as he thanked everyone for coming and encouraged them to stay for the cream tea afterwards. He was swept by an overwhelming desire to take Ellie out of there and be on their own, quiet and undisturbed.

It didn't happen of course, because he couldn't be rude. He did manage to keep hold of her hand as they made the rounds of everyone, and even sat long enough to have more tea and scones.

'You did a good job, son.' Edouard slapped his shoulder. 'I'm taking your aunt back to the cottage.' He smiled. 'We won't expect you anytime soon.

Don't worry about us.'

'Thanks, Dad.' Liam's eyes burned. 'For everything.' They didn't need to spell it out.

'Sorry to interrupt,' Harry apologised. 'The treasurer's given me the unofficial total, which doesn't include the money we've made on teas. On top of the ticket sales, a lot of people put money in the collection plates.' He grinned. 'You'll never believe it, but we've made enough to replace both windows, with money left over.'

'That's cool.' Liam playfully touched his friend's clean-shaven chin. 'Rushed into doing this, didn't you?'

A deep ruddy colour flushed his cheeks. 'Daft woman says I look a lot younger and better-looking without the beard. I reckon she needs her eyes tested.'

'Hey, if she's happy, that's all we want.'

Harry nodded. 'You're right. Do you and Ellie want to disappear?'

'That'd be great.'

'Go on, and I'll cover for you.'

'Thanks.' Liam clasped Harry's arm.

'I mean that.' He turned back to Ellie. 'You good to go?'

'I don't think we — '

'Well I do.' He quickly stood up and held out his hand to pull her to him. 'Come on, before anyone else stops us.' He made a beeline for the door, and the second they were outside he tugged off his bow tie and crammed it into his pocket.

'Where are we going, if it's not a bold question?' Ellie asked.

'The beach.'

'The beach? Dressed like this?' She pointed at his suit and then down at her own smart grey and white dress.

'Please,' he said softly, and a smile crept over her face.

'You know I can't resist when you do that.'

'What?' Liam kept walking, steering them down towards the harbour.

'Your pathetic pleading thing,' she fake-complained.

'I might be offended by that derogatory comment.'

'But you're not.' She laughed.

They hurried along the road and reached the beach where they'd first met. Liam let go of her hand and bent down to unlace his shoes.

'What're you doing?'

'What does it look like?' He tugged them off, followed by his socks. 'You told me off last time.' He shrugged off his jacket and piled it all on the nearest rock before rolling up his trousers to his knees. 'You'll spoil those pretty things.' He gestured to her elegant silver-grey shoes.

She rolled her eyes and took the shoes off, setting them carefully next to his things.

'Are we gonna be crazy together?' Liam held out his hand.

'What exactly are you asking?' Ellie's voice quavered. 'Paddling, or — '

'Paddling for right now.' Liam swallowed hard. 'A lot more very soon.'

'Oh.' Her face and neck lit up.

'I hope you're gonna choose me.' Quietly he explained his father's theory, and a slow smile crept over her face. 'Do you think I'm in with a chance?'

'I'd say you're in with a lot more than that.'

'Good, because that'll make me far happier than even this is going to.'

'What?'

Liam swept her into his arms before she realised what he had in mind, and took off running. Just because the sun had been out and it was officially May didn't mean the water was much warmer than it'd been the day they met. Ellie screamed in his ears, beating on his back and laughing as he strode in up to his knees.

'My turn to get you back for scaring me.' He kissed her, the salt spray tangy on her lips. 'I love you, Ellie Teague.'

'I love you too, you lunatic.'

'That's all I need. For always.'

'Always.' She buried her head in the crook of his neck, and Liam knew he'd do anything to keep her this way forever.

We do hope that you have enjoyed reading this large print book.

Did you know that all of our titles are available for purchase?

We publish a wide range of high quality large print books including:
**Romances, Mysteries, Classics
General Fiction
Non Fiction and Westerns**

Special interest titles available in large print are:
**The Little Oxford Dictionary
Music Book, Song Book
Hymn Book, Service Book**

Also available from us courtesy of Oxford University Press:
**Young Readers' Dictionary
(large print edition)
Young Readers' Thesaurus
(large print edition)**

For further information or a free brochure, please contact us at:
**Ulverscroft Large Print Books Ltd.,
The Green, Bradgate Road, Anstey,
Leicester, LE7 7FU, England.
Tel:** (00 44) **0116 236 4325
Fax:** (00 44) **0116 234 0205**

Other titles in the
Linford Romance Library:

CHRISTMAS AT CASTLE ELRICK

Fenella J. Miller

Severely injured in the Napoleonic Wars, Sir Ralph Elrick has been brooding in his castle for years, waiting for Miss Verity Sanderson to reach her majority and marry him. The week before Christmas, she sets off to his ancestral home to become his wife. But Castle Elrick is a cold, unwelcoming place — and Ralph and his small staff are not the only residents. Will Christmas be a joyous celebration, or will the ghosts of Castle Elrick force the newlyweds apart?